# THE LANDING PLACE

# THE LANDING PLACE

REV. SERAFIM
GASCOIGNE

Pleasant Word™
A Division of WinePress Group™
PW

Pleasant Word (a division of WinePress Publishing, PO Box 428, Enumclaw, WA 98022) functions only as book publisher. As such, the ultimate design, content, editorial accuracy, and views expressed or implied in this work are those of the author.

Unless otherwise noted, all Scriptures are taken from the *Holy Bible, New International Version®, NIV®*. Copyright © 1973, 1978, 1984 by Biblica, Inc.™ Used by permission of Zondervan. All rights reserved worldwide. WWW. ZONDERVAN.COM

Scripture references marked KJV are taken from the *King James Version* of the Bible.

Scripture references marked NASB are taken from the *New American Standard Bible*, © 1960, 1963, 1968, 1971, 1972, 1973, 1975, 1977 by The Lockman Foundation. Used by permission.

ISBN 13: 978-1-4141-1515-3
ISBN 10: 1-4141-1515-6
Library of Congress Catalog Card Number: 2009906435

# CHAPTER ONE

**N**IKOLAI'S FIRST THOUGHT was that it was simply turbulence. The SB-6 bi-plane bumped and lurched in the superheated air over the Mountain. That should have been his first warning. He pulled hard on the control stick, reining in the bucking SB-6 as if it were a Cossack steed. The plane reluctantly submitted to the young Russian pilot and finally settled on an even course at 10,000 feet.

It was then that Nikolai spotted the enemy patrol. It looked like a dark, thin snake slithering its way along the side of the Mountain just south of the Devil Rocks. *Looks like roughly 100 to 150 soldiers,* he thought. Nikolai half closed the throttle and dropped to 8,000 feet to get a closer look. From this altitude, he could now pick out a line of heavy-laden mules accompanied by armed soldiers with rifles, the sun glistening on their bayonets. The column was slowly picking its way through the rocks, twisting and turning in a long, continuous line. *It looks more like 300 at this height. Well, whatever the number, I need to get back to HQ and report this.* It would be dusk in two hours. He swung the SB-6 biplane around in a wide turn, thrusting his control stick forward for more speed, and headed northeast for the landing strip at the Aratsky Pass.

Then it happened again. The plane suddenly began to buck and sway from side to side. "What the blazes?" he shouted, his voice sounding empty against the roar of the powerful Argus engine. As if in answer, the engine spluttered and misfired in protest. The buffeting was so violent that Nikolai was forced to grip the control stick with his right hand and use his other to clutch the side of the cockpit. A cold sweat began to trickle down his back. He had flown in all types of weather during training. But this was way beyond his experience. Then as quickly as it had erupted, it was over. The plane settled down again as if nothing had happened. Nikolai blew a sigh of relief. He checked the control panel. The altimeter still read 8,000 feet. Everything appeared to be working normally. The sky was clear. The twin, snow-capped peaks of Ararat on the starboard side appeared calm and majestic against the blue September sky.

"Watch out for unexpected air pockets," Andriadi had warned him. "Always maintain a steady altitude, keeping your eyes and senses tuned to the slightest change in temperature or change of wind." He could hear his late instructor's voice clearly in his mind.

*Yeah, sure,* he thought. *But air pockets are caused by turbulent weather not by clear skies. They never told me about these kinds of air pockets at the Imperial Flying School. Well, that's one for the book,* he mused. *I can't wait to tell Smirnoff and the others when I get back.* With this thought Nikolai settled down for the flight back to base. As he looked at the calm scene below, he suddenly remembered a conversation he had had with his Azeri mechanic, Gudrat, earlier that day.

"First mission, Your Honor?"

"Yes, Gudrat! I'm flying over the Mountain. The weather looks good."

"Over the Mountain?" Gudrat's eyes registered alarm.

"Yes. Why?"

"May Allah protect you!" Gudrat took a talisman out of his pouch and offered it to Nikolai. It was a brass amulet with a sacred text from the Koran.

"Thank you, Gudrat, but I am wearing a cross my mother gave me." *That will have to do,* thought Nikolai. Besides, he was a realist. He did not hold with superstition.

When the fog came, there was no warning. Nikolai was directly over the Devil's Rocks. It sprang up like a demon from a smoke stack. It was so quick and unexpected that before he knew what was happening, it had shot upwards in white, ghostly spirals, fingering the underside of the fuselage. Nikolai immediately climbed back to 10,000 feet. "Dragon's Breath," Andriadi had called it—hot air from volcanic vents in the sides of the Mountain.

Nikolai was no fool. He knew better than to get caught in one of these death traps. He knew he must keep well clear of the billowing fog. *I need to climb and head west, away from the Mountain.* He yanked the control stick and banked the plane almost vertically to gain altitude. But however much he climbed, his SB-6 could not outrace this menace. The Dragon's Breath rose in pursuit. Within seconds the fog had rushed up and over the cockpit, completely engulfing the SB-6 and its pilot in an impenetrable, wet blanket. Nikolai was now forced to fly blind.

*Got to get out of this now!* He pulled on the control stick and gently pressed the left rudder. Instead of veering away from the fog and the Mountain, the SB-6 dropped unexpectedly. Nikolai cast a quick glance at the altimeter and noted that it read 9,000 feet. "This is not possible. I could not have lost 1,000 feet in a matter of seconds!" He removed his thick leather gauntlets and struck the glass several times with his knuckles, but the needle still pointed to 9,000. It didn't make sense. *Perhaps it is malfunctioning.* He checked the meter again. It still registered 9,000 feet. Whatever the reading, he was losing altitude fast. If he didn't correct this immediately, he risked flying into the jagged rock formations that sprung up like claws below. He pulled hard on the control-stick once more, in a desperate attempt to lift the plane. But there was no response.

Nikolai checked the altimeter again. His heart dropped. It read 8,000 feet.

He tried to pray, a thing he had only done as a child. He tried to remember a prayer. All he could remember was, "Lord have mercy! Lord have mercy!" It sounded weak. *Why should God have mercy?* Then he remembered his mother often repeating, "Spasi Bozhe! God Save me!" He began to shout out these words as he fought to right the plane.

Nikolai thought of his mother. An idiotic image came to his mind of her telling him to eat up his kasha and stop whistling through his teeth.

The blinding, wet fog buffeted and tossed his SB-6 like a predator tossing its prey before devouring it. Nikolai blew angrily through his teeth. He felt sick. It was becoming difficult to breathe. The air had turned heavy and icy. It forced itself under his goggles and into his flying suit. He felt it surging through his chest, piercing all the fibers of his body. He cried out in pain—"Spasi Bozhe!" But the cold air relentlessly burnt its way into his blood.

*Fly! Soar!* cried his mind. But Nikolai could not move. His arms had become numb. He was helpless. It was only a matter of minutes before he would smash into the rocks below. *Will death be quick? Will the SB-6 explode on impact, incinerating me in a ball of flame?*

As he huddled in the cockpit, awaiting impact, he felt a sudden, upward thrust beneath the aircraft. For a split second it seemed to arrest his descent, but then in the same moment, it began to throw him violently upwards. The upward thrust drummed and strained on the struts, making the wings quiver. *At this rate the plane will shatter at any moment.* The surging current forced and twisted the plane in a spiral up the face of Ararat. Nikolai hardly had time to realize what was happening, the movement was so swift and menacing.

He glanced once more at the altimeter. "15,000 feet," he gasped. "No one has ever flown at this height before." He watched, mesmerized, as the needle of the altimeter continued to climb. He was amazed by this reading, but not fearful. In fact, he felt a calm sweep over him as he and the SB-6 spiraled up into the rarified atmosphere. With this feeling of peace, Nikolai passed out.

# CHAPTER TWO

CAPTAIN AHMET ALI reined in his horse and stared up at the Mountain, a mixture of anticipation and dark uncertainty swirling through him. He pulled at his moustache as he pondered what to do next. *Is this my kismet?* His orders were to march to the border, bringing up the rear guard, but something else had turned up. *Is fate going to smile on me at last?* Ahmet Ali glanced up at the Mountain once more. Visibility was bad. The lower slopes were covered in a dense fogbank. But nonetheless, he had heard the plane. A plane for sure. He had heard its drone until it had suddenly cut out. There was nowhere to land. It had crashed, and he was going to find it. He would capture the pilot if he had survived the crash. If not, he would at least retrieve important intelligence information from the wreckage. Ahmet Ali frowned. *There are only two obstacles in my way; the Mountain and those rebellious fools I command. Give me regular soldiers every time, not greedy, superstitious bandits.*

The captain's mind whirled. He had orders from the Pasha. Should he ignore the crash and meet up with the main army as ordered? If he did, he would miss an opportunity to provide the Pasha with important intelligence. This would surely help him get reinstated. On the other hand, searching for the plane would put his men at risk from attack by the Kurds, apart from the hazardous nature of Ararat. He had to decide which course to take. *But which one?*

Ahmet Ali was riding ahead of the patrol that day. He wanted to be alone. Although it was unwise to travel without an escort, he needed time to think. He was not afraid of danger. *My military record is proof of that. General Mahmud Mukhtar Pasha himself awarded me a medal for bravery after the Battle of Kars.*

However, bravery had not spared Ahmet Ali banishment to the outer regions of nowhere—to the tips of the devil's horns, as the saying goes. Ahmet Ali was convinced that it was pure jealousy on the part of his fellow officers. He knew that they jokingly called him the "peacock." *What fools! They did not approve of my attention to personal appearance. Go on, fault me on strategy,* he thought bitterly. *I ride at the head of my men, not like some of you who send others to do your bidding.* "Life is not fair. But I don't complain," he muttered to himself.

Reaching a bend in the track, he stopped and dismounted, tying the reins to a stunted juniper. The fog still lay thick and impenetrable on the Mountain. *There is probably a storm stalking too,* he thought. Ahmet Ali rose to his full height and straightened his tunic. "I know you are there, and I am going to find you. I have no other choice! Fate will favor me just this once."

Sergeant Ekrem, who had been following at some distance, eventually caught up and reined in his horse beside the captain's. The sergeant dismounted and went over to where the captain was standing. Before he could say a word, Ahmet Ali waved him to silence.

"Did you hear that plane?"

"I heard a droning noise, Bey. I don't know whether it was a plane or not."

"I'm not asking you whether you think it was a plane or not," Ahmet Ali hissed. "Did you hear it?"

"Yes, Bey."

"Do you know what that means?"

The sergeant chewed his lip. He avoided the captain's eyes, looking at his horse as if the answer to the question lay there. "No, I don't, Bey."

"Ah, I am surrounded by fools! It means an enemy pilot is up there somewhere in that fog." Ahmet Ali fingered his holster as he looked up at the dense blanket on the slope above. "I intend to find him!"

# CHAPTER TWO

Ahmet Ali had been surrounded by fools ever since he took command of guarding the eastern lands of the Turkish Empire. What else could he expect from peasant soldiers and cutthroat mercenaries? But they were not the only fools. He had to put up with the fools at Command HQ. And now, here in this wilderness, he was trying to make plans that depended on the dull-witted sergeant and the undisciplined mercenaries. *No. Forget Ekrem. The sergeant will never dare to reveal his true opinion. He will always agree, even if he doesn't.* Ahmet Ali scowled, untied his horse, and climbed back into his saddle. *The mercenaries are a different matter.*

The sergeant's horse began to get restless, stamping its hind feet on the rough stones of the trail. Ekrem too shifted on his feet uneasily as he tried to calm his mount. He looked up at the captain. "I have to report, Bey, that one of the Azeris, Tabrik, spotted something following us!"

Ahmet Ali glared down at Ekrem. "Something? What do you mean 'something'? What was it, Man?"

"Tabrik did not know who or what it was, but he was sure that we were being followed."

"But if he didn't see anything, how did he know we were being followed? What is this nonsense?"

The sergeant fell silent.

"I want facts, Sergeant!" Ahmet Ali pulled at his moustache and gave Ekrem a black look. "Did Tabrik see anything? Did he hear anything? If not, then don't waste my time with stories!"

Of all the mercenaries, Tabrik was not to be trusted. Ahmet Ali had not forgotten the murder of the German botanist six months ago. Tabrik had shot the German for his buttons, which the Azeri took to be gold. They turned out to be brass buttons. Ahmet Ali had discovered these brass buttons fixed to the saddle of Tabrik's horse. When he asked Tabrik how he came by them, Tabrik replied that he had found an old jacket caught in a thorn bush. He said it was too torn to be useful, but he had removed the buttons and decorated his saddle with them. He said that at first he mistook the buttons for gold, but on closer examination, realized that they were made of brass.

Ahmet Ali had heard Tabrik boasting in his own dialect to a fellow Azeri how he had shot the stranger for the gold on his jacket. The captain knew enough Azeri to understand what he had said, but decided to let the matter rest. It would be impossible to convict the man of murder, although he had boasted about it to another Azeri. Should he have executed Tabrik on the spot? But shooting an Azeri would only have made matters worse. *I should have arrested the bandit and handed him over to the Turkish gendarmerie.* But if he had done that, he would have risked reprisal from Tabrik's fellow clansmen.

News of the killing of the German botanist had eventually reached the Porte and then the German embassy. Was that why Ahmet Ali had not been reinstated? Was he being blamed for the death of the German? There was nothing he could do to prove that this Azeri was the killer. And there had been an international uproar since Germany was an ally of Turkey. A force of heavily armed gendarmes was sent to the area to retrieve the body and to punish the wrongdoers. After several months of investigation, the case was dropped due to lack of evidence. *Why did no one ask me what had happened?*

The sergeant stood waiting, a blank expression on his face. *Better to send Ekrem ahead with the main patrol. I will have to do the job myself. But I will need help from the Azeri scouts. What if they won't cooperate? I have no other choice. It seems it is my kismet to have to rely on murderers and thieves.*

Ahmet Ali paused and threw a sideways glance. The main body of the patrol was still some distance behind on the track. "It was a plane, I'm telling you! It's crashed up on the Mountain."

"Yes, Bey."

The captain cupped his hands and scanned the slope above. "It must have crashed somewhere in that fogbank. I need to investigate." He looked back down the track. The patrol was now approaching, led by the chief Azeri scout, Javad.

Javad, a surly-looking Azeri, pulled up his horse, dismounted, and came up to the captain. He carried a Turkish Mauser rifle slung across his back. As he approached the captain, he squinted as if he were not accustomed to the bright sun. He covered his eyes with one hand, peering at the captain from eyes as black as deep pools. There was a deep scar above his left eyebrow. His face reminded Ahmet Ali of an ancient Persian warrior he had seen on a frieze from Persepolis. As he drew nearer to Ahmet Ali, a small owl suddenly flew out of nowhere, passing swiftly between them, and landed several yards away under a rock. The Azeri jumped back in surprise. The captain simply stared after it. Then turning to the Azeri he said, "Ah, Javad, I am going to need you to select twenty men for me."

"Yes, Offendi. But what for?"

"An enemy plane has crashed somewhere up in the fogbank." The captain pointed to the fog-laded slope above them. "Somewhere up there is a plane and possibly a pilot who needs to be interrogated…."

The Azeri looked in the direction the captain was pointing. "But, Offendi, he's most likely dead if he crashed there."

"Well, whether he's dead or not, we need to search the area. There will be maps, military orders, and other intelligence information that we need to find. I want you to select twenty men for the search."

The Azeri fell silent.

"Well?"

"We'll be asking for trouble from the local tribesmen."

"That's why I want a few men." Ahmet Ali gave the scout a venomous look.

"We can investigate without making it obvious." He paused. "If there's trouble, the main patrol can come to our rescue. We have handled the Kurds before."

"But, Offendi, it's not just the Kurds that are the problem. I am certain we can handle them. It's…"

"Well?"

"We can't go up there. The mountain is forbidden to us!"

"What do you mean 'forbidden'?"

"It's forbidden, Offendi."

"Why?"

Javad seemed reluctant to give an answer. He looked at Ahmet Ali with open mouth, as if to say, *What kind of stupid question is that?*

"Tell me why it is forbidden!"

Javad looked at the sergeant for support. Ekrem kept his eyes fixed on the ground.

Finally, Javad pointed up at the fogbank as if to confirm his fears. "The Mountain of Nuh can't be climbed. Those who try, meet a fearful end. It will always keep its secret."

"What secret?"

"A secret, which only Allah knows."

"Then how do you know it's a secret? Secrets are for assassins and conspirators."

This remark was lost on the Azeri.

"It is a holy mountain." The Azeri's voice rose in pitch. "The Koran says the Mountain is the landing place of the ark of Nuh. It is forbidden for anyone to climb the Mountain."

"It's forbidden, you say. It's a secret. Who says so?"

"It is the will of Allah that the Mountain should keep its secret."

"To climb the Holy Mountain is to lose one's soul," added the sergeant.

"What nonsense is that?" exploded the captain. "That's just an old woman's tale. Surely you don't believe that?"

Javad and Sergeant Ekrem did not answer.

The Captain knew very well that his own Turkish troops and Javad and the rest of the Azeris did believe that. He had thought for a moment that he could overcome their superstition by reasoning with them. But obviously that was not going to work. He would have to find another way around this obstacle. If not, his plan would be in jeopardy, and all because of some superstition about the Mountain. He had come across it before, but at that time it had not impeded his plans. Now it was different. He could order all he liked, but the Azeris would not budge an inch. He looked at each man in turn. If he was not going to win them over by force or argument, then he had to think of a way around the superstitious fears of the patrol.

"The men will not climb, Offendi." Javad added, "They fear the Shaytan."

"The Shaytan? What on earth is that?"

"It is an evil spirit, Offendi, that sucks the soul out of a man like a spider feasting on a fly."

"What is worse," Sergeant Ekrem added, "is that the man does not die but is forced to wander the slopes of the Mountain like a wild animal."

"Nonsense!" The captain had heard enough. *How can these men be so ignorant?* "What kind of grown men are you to believe the tales we tell children to frighten them?"

"It is true!" Javad turned to the sergeant.

"He's right, Bey."

Ahmet Ali prided himself on his powers of persuasion. In his eyes, he was no fool. He could see that the sergeant and the Azeri scout believed without a shadow of doubt the legend of the forbidden mountain. For them, Ararat was a living nightmare. It was real. The mountain punished those who dared to commit such sacrilege by attempting to climb it. He had to find another way to persuade them. Challenging their superstition was not going to change their minds. He would have to acknowledge their fear and appear sympathetic. Turning to the men, he said in a quieter voice, "I understand your respect for the Mountain…. but I think it is only forbidden to climb the higher slopes, where the ark might be. Surely the lower slopes are not forbidden? If they were, the nomads would not graze their sheep there. They would not do that if there was any risk of punishment. " The captain turned and pointed up at the fogbank. "I don't believe it applies to that area up there. That's where I believe the plane crashed."

The Azeri silently ran his hand up to the trigger of his Mauser. The captain instinctively responded by resting his hand on his open holster. He drew himself up to his full height in his saddle. "I need to find that plane—there's important information that I need to pass onto the Pasha." The captain paused. "Besides, the Pasha will reward us handsomely for this," he said smiling. "We'll simply search the slope below the fogbank. Just think of the reward!"

Javad stared hard at the fogbank for a few minutes. Then he turned to Ahmet Ali and grinned.

"I'll need a detachment of twenty mounted men. See to it!"

The Azeri remounted and saluted the captain in a sloppy manner. He turned his horse and rode off down the track to the main body of the patrol. Sergeant Ekrem waited to receive further orders.

Ahmet Ali sat and watched the Azeri ride back down the track, and then he turned to the sergeant. "There might be more planes. Perhaps the Imperial Air Force is planning to attack us from the rear." Ahmet Ali scanned the sky above Ararat.

"Yes, Bey."

"I need to stay behind and find that plane." The captain straightened his tunic and rose up in the stirrups. He was a tall, imposing figure as he towered over the shorter sergeant. "Get the men ready to move on. I want you to meet up with the main army in two days."

"That's going to be a hard drive, Bey."

"Hard drive or not, I expect you to do it! You will report to the Pasha, telling him that I have stayed behind to collect important intelligence on the enemy."

"Yes, Bey!"

Sergeant Ekrem saluted the captain, mounted his horse, and rode back towards the patrol. He was not pleased with the task ahead of him and unhappy that he had not been able to convince the captain that Tabrik, who had brought up the rear of the patrol, had sensed a presence following them. The other men had felt it, too.

The sergeant did not relish the thought of having to report directly to the Pasha. The Pasha was not an easy man. In fact, he was cruel and irascible. He was known for punishing those who brought him bad news. He would most likely punish the sergeant for simply bearing the news that Captain Ahmet Ali had stayed behind. No, he was not happy with his orders.

Meanwhile, the captain dismounted. He tied his horse to the branch of an oak that stood like a lone sentinel, pointing ominously to the Mountain as if to say, *That's where you have to go....But don't say I didn't warn you.* Ahmet Ali shrugged his shoulders. For a moment a shadow passed over his mind. *I am getting jumpy like those superstitious fools I am forced to command. I must concentrate on the task at hand. This is, after all, my kismet. Yes! I will soon bid farewell to this desolate, inhospitable region.*

*I will regain favor once more with the Pasha. I will show my fellow officers that I am the better man after all.*

Ahmet Ali had been unfairly relieved of his position at staff headquarters. He had boasted to his fellow officers that he was connected, however somewhat spuriously, to his hero, General Ahmed Mukhtar Pasha. This famous general had been sent at the outbreak of the Russo-Turkish War in 1878 to take charge of military operations in Erzurum. Although the Russians eventually defeated the Turkish Army, Mukhtar's victories against the Russians on the eastern front won him the title *Ghazi*—the Victorious. Ahmet Ali's "connection" was that he had served as a young subaltern under the general's nephew, Mahmud Mukhtar Pasha.

Ahmet Ali counted proximity to this military family as some kind of blood relationship. He was very fond of bragging that General Mukhtar had been made Grand Vizier after the war, as if it made his "connection" even more significant. The other field commanders were tired of his bragging and bombastic manner, so they had decided to get rid of "Captain Peacock."

It was true that Ahmet Ali had an obsession about his appearance. Even after an arduous ride across rough country, he would appear neat and clean at the end of the day—with not a hair out of place. His riding boots were always highly polished, and his Smith and Wesson .44 rimfire revolver gleamed from constant polishing. The captain kept a special silk cloth in his holster for this purpose.

Ahmet Ali crossed the narrow track and climbed up onto a large boulder. From there he had a more expansive view of the Mountain. It would be easier to plan his route to find the wreckage from this vantage point. *In contrast to the heat-heavy stupor of this arid, brown wasteland with its incessant cacophony of cicadas and flies, the upper slope will offer a refreshing change.* There, despite the heavy fog, was an emerald world of silence and cool air. There, nothing seemed to move, and not even the smallest sound disturbed the absolute calm. *It will be good, too, to get out of this persistent dry wind that fills the nostrils with dust.* Before swallowing water, Ahmet Ali frequently had to wash out his mouth to get rid of the grit. *Yes, up there on the sheep-cropped slopes, it will be different.*

*We will travel on foot if necessary.* The captain observed that there were two tracks winding their way up the steep slope. One could be traveled on horseback, the other was too steep and narrow for horses. He decided on the more accessible track. *Yes, if necessary, we will dismount if it becomes too steep for the horses.*

# CHAPTER THREE

JAVAD RETURNED TO the main body of the patrol. This consisted of 200 men. Of these, 30 were mounted troops, mainly mercenaries drawn from the Caucasus and Turks from the Kayseri region. There were two Turkish corporals in charge of the foot soldiers. Sergeant Ekrem commanded the mounted troops, from which Javad was to select 20 men. These would be mostly Azeris. These men knew the area well. When they were not serving the Turkish Army as mercenaries, they hunted for game and, on occasion, robbed and slew unsuspecting travelers. They were ruthless killers. The first mercenary that came to mind was Tabrik. He was their best marksman. However Javad knew the captain would not be pleased with this choice.

Javad went in search of his cousin, Vugor. He found him sitting by a campfire, cleaning his Mauser. Vugor looked up and grinned when he saw Javad. Although they were cousins, Vugor did not resemble Javad in any way. He was short and thickset. His head was shaven and almost perfectly round, like a cannon ball. There was hardly any sign of a cranium. His head appeared to sit directly on his shoulders as if he had no neck, and his face was pock-marked and sallow. He spoke with an unpleasant nasal rasp, which made his speech sound menacing.

Both Javad and Vugor were seasoned scouts, familiar with the terrain, although they had never dared to climb Ararat itself. They were also experienced hunters. It was rumored that Javad's acute and fine-tuned hearing could distinguish the movement of his prey from that of the wind. They had a long family history as mercenaries for the Ottomans. Javad decided it would be best to choose men who were related. This would ensure their reliability in battle, should they meet up with Mountain Kurds.

Javad laid out the captain's plans before Vugor.

"I don't like it, Javad. We are hunters, not scavengers!" "I don't like it much either." Javad smiled "Then on the other hand, think of the reward."

"Think of the punishment, you mean."

"There's no risk of punishment if we keep to the lower slopes. Just a day's work and we will be rich."

"No one climbs the Mountain."

"We will not be climbing the Mountain itself."

"I still don't like it. The captain is too fond of taking risks."

"Well, I like a man who is willing to take risks."

"He'll get us killed." Vugor spat on the ground. "We should kill him first."

"Then we would have the whole Ottoman army against us. I don't want to spend the rest of my life hunting for hares. I want gold and honor. I want to be around to enjoy my great grandchildren"

"I say slit his throat and dump his body for the ravens. We can say the Mountain Kurds got him."

"And you think we'll go unpunished? The Pasha is not that stupid." Javad laughed at his own words.

"We'll be punished by the Mountain," said Vugor.

Javad laid his hand reassuringly on Vugor's shoulder. "Look, my brother, it's a risk, I agree. But as the captain says, there are nomads up there all the time, and they don't come under the curse."

"That's because they are guardians of the Holy Mountain."

"That's what they may think," laughed Javad. "Anyway, I can't see any harm in searching the lower slopes as the captain suggests. At the first sign of trouble we can quit."

"Well if there is a reward…" Vugor smiled.

"And let's make that the goal of the search. I don't want the others to think about the Mountain. The less they think about it, the quicker the job." Javad stared at Vugor. "Remember—only the reward."

"Don't fret. We have cut bread and salt together." Vugor gave his cousin an ugly look.

Javad went and selected twenty men, including Tabrik. He told them the captain's plan, emphasizing that there would be a considerable reward. "All we have to do is find the plane. We will have to watch out for Mountain Kurds, but we do that anyway."

"But what about the Mountain?" asked several of the men.

"We won't go anywhere near the Mountain itself. Besides, we can get there and back in a single day if the weather holds out," Javad assured them.

"I don't think so." Vugor muttered under his breath.

Within minutes Javad returned to Ahmet Ali with Vugor and twenty other men, both Azeris and Asiatic Russians. Fear showed in their eyes, but their greed had driven them to volunteer to climb the lower slopes of the Mountain.

The captain studied the volunteers lined up before him. "We'll need to keep our wits about us. We may run into nomads, but we can deal with them if we have to. That's a risk we have to take." He looked at Javad for support.

"I'll tell you right now, there's an element of risk. But the reward will be far greater."

Javad smiled. "If it works, it'll be yogurt, Offendi." The scout turned to Vugor. "If not, curds! Either way, we have nothing to lose, except some time —and that's your problem, Offendi."

Ahmet Ali frowned at the impertinence of the scout but said nothing. "And the sooner my reward," he added under his breath. He stroked his moustache and then turned to address the other men. "No time for playing the gavel in paradise. Drum up the men, and let's set out in one hour."

Javad laughed. "I'm no musician, Offendi."

"You're not kidding, Javad. You couldn't beat time to a dirge," Vugor said, a sarcastic grin on his face.

Javad spun around and confronted his cousin. It looked to the captain like there was going to be a nasty incident. That was the last thing he needed at this time.

There was an awkward pause as both men sized each other up. Then as the captain stepped forward, his revolver cocked for action, both scouts burst into laughter, slapping and punching each other playfully. The rest of the men hooted and laughed at the spectacle.

The captain did not find the standoff amusing, but he constrained his anger. He knew that humor was sometimes necessary to keep the morale high and maintain control of his band of undisciplined ruffians. They were often amused by Ahmet Ali's use of Azeri expressions. However he had to show caution—humor not frivolity. He had to maintain their respect at all costs. He dare not appear a fool before his men. If he did that, he would lose them. He would most likely end up with his throat cut and his body left for carrion on the side of the Mountain.

The track allowed for riders, up to a point. However it soon became too narrow and steep. The men were forced to dismount and lead their horses.

"I don't like it. We're not meant to be here," muttered one of the Asiatic Russians.

"Well, don't let Javad or Vugor hear that," warned his companion, "or you'll have more to fear than the curse of the Mountain."

Javad and Vugor walked with their horses a few yards behind the captain.

"He's mad you know," Vugor whispered. "He'll get us all killed."

"Mad he may be, but he's an experienced soldier," Javad replied, not looking at his companion. "Keep your voice down. We don't want the others to hear."

"I think we should kill him before he kills us with his crazy plans," said Vugor, looking around cautiously. "We can say the Kurds got him."

"Hold your tongue, Vugor. Don't you want the reward?"

"Not if my widow gets to spend it!"

Javad laughed and prodded Vugor in the ribs with his elbow. "You selfish goat!"

Vugor did not react to Javad's taunts, but fell silent. Javad could tell that Vugor was not amused, that he meant what he said. *When Vugor broods, that means trouble*, thought Javad. "Whatever you're thinking, don't," he warned.

Meanwhile the sun had faded into a blur behind the northern peak of Ararat, leaving a golden sliver around the silhouette of the peak. The air was turning colder, and there was a damp stillness settling over the rocks and stunted oaks, which now appeared gray and dull in the fading light. A heavy mist began to descend from the slopes above. Soon it would envelope them, too.

Ahmet Ali looked back at the men following. The young Mahmud was bringing up the rear. Being the youngest of the group he had been laden with extra rations, like a village mule. It looked like he was cursing to himself as he followed the file up the narrow track.

It was now necessary to find somewhere to rest. The mist had thickened considerably. They would not be able to proceed in such conditions. The captain held up his arm and signaled the contingent to halt. "We'll stop here, until the mist lifts. Don't want to go blundering over the edge." For the last fifteen minutes they had been following the edge of the Ahora Gorge. There was a long drop into the Gorge below. One false move, even in good visibility, meant death for the careless.

Ahmet Ali watched as Vugor went back down the track to Mahmud. The latter was cursing at an older Azeri who was trying to untie a sack from Mahmud's horse.

"What are you doing? This is my load. What do you want?"

The older Azeri ignored the younger and continued to untie a small sack that dangled from the saddle.

"What's in it?"

The older Azeri continued to ignore the younger as if he were of less importance than the horse. He seemed intent on removing the sack. He didn't even bother to look up, but said in an abrupt manner, "Loosen the rope the other side!"

Mahmud fiercely turned on him. "Eat a little less, and hire yourself a servant. Don't order me around. Do it yourself. I'm not your slave."

The older man suddenly paused. Then as swift as a viper, he pulled out a knife and struck at the younger man. In the same instant Vugor threw himself on the older man, gripping his wrists and forcing him to drop the knife. It clattered on the stony ground. The older Azeri glared at Mahmud but said nothing. He looked at Vugor and then once more at Mahmud and spat on the ground.

Mahmud leapt at the man. His reaction was so immediate that he sent the older man sprawling under the horse. The animal shied and kicked out nervously.

Vugor grabbed the bridle, steadying the horse, and shouted out an order. Both men stopped in their tracks. The older Azeri got to his feet, dusted himself down, then walked up the track in silence. Meanwhile Mahmud began to unload some of his equipment as if nothing had happened. Vugor said not another word and followed the older Azeri up the track.

Ahmet Ali never ceased to be amazed at how a fight could be stopped by a single order from either Vugor or Javad. He did not understand these orders, although he had a fair knowledge of Azeri. He could never work out how they had such an effect on the other men, but they did. Even a look from either of them would often settle a dispute.

The patrol set up a temporary camp while they waited for the fog to lift. The captain ordered rations to be distributed to the men. Javad handed out strips of dried goat's meat and bread rusks—not very appetizing fare, but sufficient for the climb ahead of them. As the men sat on the rocks on the side of the track or stood with their horses, the fog came down like a thick blanket, completely obliterating the terrain around them. It was so thick that Ahmet Ali could only see as far as his horse, tethered a few feet from him at the side of the track. Its ears lay flat back on its head. The animal was restless, stamping it hooves in expectation. Beyond his horse, all he could see were the smudged outlines of rocks and trees and the ghostly figures of the men.

An unearthly silence hung in the air. Only the sound of horses panting and the men talking amongst themselves reminded Ahmet Ali that he was not alone on the Mountain. Javad had warned him that to move even a few feet was dangerous in such conditions. Now he understood what Javad meant. *Nothing to do but wait.* The wet fog clung to his clothes; the moisture seemed to penetrate into his bones. Everything was cold and damp, the fog silvering the stunted acacia with droplets. Ahmet Ali could hear the blood pulsating through his head. His breathing suddenly sounded loud in the silence. He felt as if something was trying to penetrate his pores, to enter into his bones and freeze the marrow. *This is no ordinary fog. It visits fear upon both men and horses.*

Ahmet Ali could hear the men beginning to mutter prayers, clutching, he was sure, at their talismans. *They must think this is the dreaded Shaytan, the malevolent spirit that lives deep inside the Holy Mountain.* Even the pragmatic captain sensed a menace in this flesh-chilling mist. He instinctively fingered his revolver in its holster and scanned the area on all sides, almost expecting a surprise attack from someone or something unknown.

As quickly as the mist had descended, it suddenly lifted, blown away by some invisible force, like steam from a kettle. It drifted off to envelope another area of the slope to the west of their position. The mist's lifting revealed twilight on the Mountain. Ahmet Ali looked around. Mahmud crouched fetal-like, obviously paralyzed with fear. The horses and the men all huddled together like threatened sheep.

# CHAPTER FOUR

NIKOLAI WAS RUDELY brought back to consciousness by a shuddering and spluttering from the powerful Argus engine. Before he realized what was happening, the rhythmic throbbing of the engine fell silent. The SB-6 suddenly became a suicidal crow, plummeting and diving without warning towards the jagged rocks below. The freezing air screamed through the struts of the wings like a thousand sirens, luring him into the side of the Mountain below. Cross currents buffeted and tore at the fabric. *I must not allow myself to fall into a helpless spiral. I need to think fast. I need to volplane.* Andriadi had trained him to drop from 5,000 feet with cut-off engine. He had been successful, even commended for his skill at landing in this manner. That had been a test, a part of his pilot's diploma. This was for real. After several grueling minutes, Nikolai managed to pull the plane out of the dive. Although totally blinded by the fog, he was now gliding down instead of dropping like a stone.

Then all of a sudden he saw a gap in the fog. In desperation, he flung the control-stick hard to the left, and holding up the plane's nose with the right rudder, he dropped into a vertical sideslip towards the hole. All his learning and skill were being put to the test. *What would Andriadi do?* Within seconds he had entered the hole, where to his amazement he saw he was over the Ahora glacier, which he had passed hours before on his return flight to base. Directly below, the glacier crept down the Mountain, a spread of ice and rock. To the west of the glacier was a frozen lake, bordered by an embankment of solid ice and snow. *If I can steer towards this lake at the edge of the glacier, I might be able to land on its smooth surface.*

Nikolai pulled hard on the stick. He was going to crash nose first if he didn't get the plane parallel with the ground. At the last moment he straightened out, the SB-6 coming down swiftly, touching the frozen lake with a thud, and for a moment rearing up like a startled stallion. It skidded sideways on impact, slipping and spinning around on its own length. His momentum carried him into the ice embankment at the rim of the frozen lake, the grinding of the undercarriage jarring through his body the whole way. There was an angry screech for a split second as the plane crashed into the ice. Then there was an unearthly silence.

Nikolai could hear his own breathing. A pulse in his neck quivered fitfully. He sat there dazed and bruised in the battered cockpit. *Thank God the SB-6 was fitted with a reinforced undercarriage.* Had it been otherwise, the plane would have broken up and Nikolai with it. He assessed his body for injuries; he was bruised but not seriously injured. *No bones broken.* His heavy leather helmet and suit had taken most of the impact. His hands, however, were swollen and cut. In his preoccupation with trying to land, he had forgotten to put on his gauntlets again. He felt no pain; they were numb. *I must have smashed them on the control panel on impact.*

For a false moment Nikolai felt that the ordeal was over. But seeing the wrecked cockpit around him brought him back to reality. All around was silence. The fog was beginning to drift higher. His flying suit was drenched with moisture, and the air was freezing. Nikolai tried to take stock of his situation, but his mind was numb. He felt exhaustion overwhelming him. *The sub-zero temperature will finish me off in a matter of minutes!* In desperation, Nikolai scanned the frozen terrain for some form of shelter. *If I can find an ice hole, I might be able to recover my strength.* He knew that Parrott, the explorer, had survived this way.

As he surveyed the scene around him, he caught a glimpse of something out of the corner of his eye. It looked like a figure of a huge man standing at the end of the frozen lake. But as he swung around, removing his goggles to look closer, it was gone.

# CHAPTER FOUR

He clutched the sides with his bruised hands and pulled himself slowly out of the cockpit, sliding painfully down the fuselage. Every bone in his body ached. Although it appeared that his legs had not been injured, he felt unsure of his balance, and it was all he could do to stagger a few feet from the plane. He was finally forced to sit on the ground. *I can't stay here. Every minute counts. I must find shelter.* He looked back for a moment at his SB-6. It lay on the ice, a crumpled tangle of wire and metal.

Nikolai staggered to his feet with great difficulty. The pain in his legs took his breath away. He swayed as he regained his balance and then stood poised for a few seconds, like a child taking its first steps. Then, leaning on the side of the ice mound, he shuffled along its edge, hoping to find a gap in the ice bank. All around him was bleak silence, save for his own crunching footsteps.

He had only gone a little way when a bitter gust of wind began to blow down from the slopes above the frozen lake. It rushed against him. He wrapped his scarf around his face so that he could breathe in the frozen air. He felt vulnerable and inconsequential against the vastness of the Mountain. His eyelashes began to ice up, and his eyes felt frozen. It was difficult to focus. He knew time was running out. He had to force his feet to walk over the frozen ground; stopping now would mean the end for him. And yet he had to pause for a few seconds to avoid falling from exhaustion. He steadied himself once more and summoned up the strength to go on.

He had only gone a few more yards when he stopped and stared in disbelief at the scene in front of him. Near the lake's overflow, there was a gap, but it wasn't a natural hole in the ice. It was a huge, man-made entrance to what looked like a gigantic wooden hangar, half submerged in the ice. *But who would keep airplanes up here on the Mountain? And who would risk building a landing strip near an unstable glacier? Am I hallucinating?* He closed his eyes, trying to refocus, and then looked again. It was no illusion. There before him stood an enormous wooden structure. It was tilted to one side, and Nikolai was able to see its roof, partly protruding from its entombment in the ice. His gaze fell upon a flat catwalk that ran down the length of the top of the structure. Its immense size amazed Nikolai. The hangar, for what else could it be, was as long as a city block in St. Petersburg. As he approached he could see clearly that the entrance was a great doorway, nearly twenty feet square, with one door missing.

Nikolai shivered in the bitter wind. This was no ice hole, and the interior would probably be no warmer than the outside; but at least inside he would be screened from the wind. There were ten yards of slippery ascent before he could reach the entrance. *Well, here goes,* he thought as he staggered and side-slipped up the last few yards to the great entrance of the strange building. To steady himself, Nikolai leaned against one of the posts of the doorway. He noticed that its surface was highly polished. It was covered with a wax-like paint. It reminded him of shellac.

Once inside, he moved away from the entrance and leaned, panting, against the wall. Here too the surface was highly polished and slippery. Someone had painstakingly covered the wood with wax. The floor beneath his feet was made of rough planks. It was covered with a solid layer of grime He removed his scarf and was immediately conscious of a sweet smell. He peered into the darkness, but could see nothing. The light reflecting from the ice only lit the entrance way. *This is no hangar. There are no residues of petrol or oil or aircraft paint, all the familiar smells associated with aviation. It is something other.*

On closer examination Nikolai noticed that the wood used to build this strange refuge was familiar, but in his confused state, he could not identify it. In sheer exhaustion, he sank to the floor, sliding down the shiny surface of the wall behind him.

# CHAPTER FIVE

"JAVAD!" CALLED THE captain.

The Azeri scout stood up, stepped out of the group of huddled men, and came quickly up to Ahmet Ali.

"There's still enough light to see by. We need to move on."

Javad's face was grim. "We can't expect the men to camp on the Mountain."

"I wasn't suggesting that. I want to search the immediate area before it gets too dark, and then we can set up camp farther down, among the oaks."

By this time the men were up and tending to their horses. They were unusually silent. There was none of the loud bravado that normally accompanied their actions. The men, when they did speak, spoke in whispers, as if fearful of being heard or disturbing something that should not be disturbed.

Ahmet Ali had been brought up a secular Turk. He had been circumcised according to the tradition of his faith, but that was the only time he had entered a mosque. He was not overly superstitious, nor did he believe in the supernatural. Yet here on the Mountain he felt threatened, although he did not show it, as if something were trying to force its way into his very being. *The sooner we find the plane and beat retreat the better,* he thought. Despite his military expertise and training, he realized that this was a situation that he might not be able to control.

He was dealing with something beyond his experience. He took out his revolver and released the safety catch.

Javad and Vugor were checking each man and his horse.

"Where's Yusef?" one of the men cried.

"Where's Mutar?" cried another.

Two horses were standing unattended, still tethered as they had been before the descent of the heavy fog. Vugor spat on the ground in anger, "They should know better than to leave the track."

"They stayed with the horses," said another Azeri.

"Well, they are not there now!" Vugor snarled.

The men began running to and fro, calling for the missing men. Their voices echoed mockingly across the Gorge.

The Captain addressed Javad. "Who's missing?"

"It's one of the Russians and that old fool, Yusef," replied Javad. "Where could they have gone?" He fell silent. Fear was in his eyes.

At that moment Vugor came back, carrying two bags belonging to the missing men. "They apparently didn't camp with the other men, otherwise they would be here now." Vugor threw the packs on the ground in front of Ahmet Ali.

"What's happened?" Mahmud asked, joining the captain and the two scouts.

Javad looked at Mahmud but did not answer.

Mahmud suddenly turned pale and stared at the ground. "It's the Shaytan," he whispered.

"Nonsense!" barked the captain.

Vugor stared angrily at the captain. "And we'll be next!"

Ahmet Ali's worst fear was becoming a reality. This wild, fearless band of cutthroats was on the verge of turning into cringing cowards if he did not take command of the situation. He had to think quickly. *For all their hardened and callous exteriors, they fear the Shaytan, who they believe lives in the volcanic vents of the Mountain and who roams the slopes of Ararat seeking souls to devour. They believe that anyone daring to climb this forbidden ground would perish in this frightful manner.* The captain pondered again how this did not make sense since the nomads grazed their flocks of goats and sheep up there. *How is it that they are not affected?* He had asked Javad this question many times.

A murmur rippled through the patrol. The captain made an effort to calm the men. "They wandered off in the fog and are probably on their way back at this very moment." He needed time to think. *Where have those fools gone?*

Then all of a sudden pandemonium broke out. The men began to shout and curse.

"It's the Shaytan. It has got Yusef and that Russian!" The men cocked their Mausers in desperation. "We'll be next if we don't get off the Mountain!"

"We've come this far; we are not turning back," ordered the captain. "We must go on! Javad! You tell them!"

The scout stared back at the captain in silence.

"Surely you don't believe in all this superstitious nonsense?" The captain stared at Javad. The scout was sweating profusely. Ahmet Ali had never seen Javad in such a state of fear. Here was a hardened mercenary— a tough, ruthless killer—trembling like a frightened youth.

"That was no ordinary fog, Offendi. I've been in thicker fog many times. This was different."

"How?"

"It seemed to seep into my body, as if searching for my soul."

Vugor nodded in agreement.

"So we are going to be scared off the Mountain by a ghost?" *Appealing to their greed might bring the situation to order.* "Think of the reward!"

But it was to no avail. Fear had overtaken the patrol, including the scouts—men who feared no one. Here they were dealing with the unknown. There was nothing more Ahmet Ali could do. They could not go on.

"We'll camp farther down, among those oaks," Ahmet Ali said calmly.

Javad looked at the captain and then at Vugor.

"Tomorrow at first light we'll scour the lower slopes." The captain said this merely to calm the men. He knew they would most likely have to climb much higher if his prediction was correct. The plane had crashed farther up. Of that he was sure. If necessary, he would go alone. He was not going to ignore this opportunity or let this riff-raff weaken his determination. *Can I prevail on Javad's greed? If so, Vugor will probably follow suit. The others would be useful but not as skilled as the two scouts. If the wreckage is to be found, Javad and Vugor will find it.*

That night the captain hardly slept. He had to find a way to convince the scouts, and if possible, some of the men, to continue the search for the downed plane. *How to overcome their fear by greed—that is the question. What can I offer them that they can't refuse? Gold, power…? What would matter most to Javad? Power, respect…gold? Yes, that's it. Of course they are greedy for gold, but respect is worth much more. I will tell Javad, "You will not only be handsomely paid, but also you will be appointed chief scout of the Sultan's army in this region. Think of what that would mean for your family honor, for the honor of your clan!"* If this did not work, then Ahmed Ali would have to challenge his courage. "Javad is a brave warrior, an outstanding and accomplished scout. But Javad is afraid of ghosts!" This would be a terrible risk to take, but the captain had no other choice.

At first light, Ahmed Ali awoke. He had only snatched a few hours of sleep, spending most of the night thinking about his predicament. The question still raced through his mind: *How do I overcome the superstition of the Azeris. On all accounts, I must show no fear or weakness when I confront Javad.* The first rays of the sun touched the Mountain, turning its peak from the gray of first light into a splash of brilliant gold.

All of the captain's thinking and planning paid off. Javad was scared, but his ego, his sense of personal honor, would carry him through the coming ordeal. The captain had said very little. Javad had slept on it, too. He said he would not allow himself to be labeled a coward. And just as Ahmed Ali expected, Vugor followed Javad. In fact, most of the men, with obvious prompting or threatening from Javad, agreed to continue the search now that it was daylight. Those who did not want to go on packed their mounts and descended silently, like dejected dogs, back down the Mountain. They were finished in Ahmed Ali's eyes.

# CHAPTER SIX

NIKOLAI WAS JOLTED awake by a bright light shining in his face. He turned his head away and slowly opened his eyes. It was bright sunlight reflecting off the rocks around him. He had been in a strange dream. Someone with powerful arms had lifted him up from where he lay in the darkness of the strange hangar and had carried him gently outside and across the frozen lake.

Nikolai had not seen a face, but he was aware that the person who carried him was tall and very strong. He had held Nikolai's body tightly against his chest. It smelled musty, like damp blankets and rotting hay. Intense warmth radiated from the stranger. It seeped into the sinews of Nikolai's body, as if to protect him from the bitter wind. That was all he could remember. Now he was awake, lying on a rocky hillside with the reflection of the sun shining in his eyes. He closed his eyes again. *Am I still dreaming?*

Suddenly he became conscious of a presence. He was not alone. Slowly he opened his eyes again and found a beautiful face gazing down at him. For a moment he thought he had died and was seeing an angelic being. Green eyes looked deep into his. *You are safe, it's over,* they seemed to say. He made a feeble effort to sit up. An arm firmly supported him, but his body shook with pain. He leaned back, and the arm brought him gently to the ground. Nikolai just lay there. He was content to gaze at the face above him, which was framed by long, black hair that tumbled down around her face and shoulders.

After a few minutes, Nikolai regained his strength sufficiently to sit up. Before him knelt a young woman about his height and age. She wore a long, voluminous, dull brown skirt that billowed behind her. Her blouse was made of a coarse, gray cotton, over which she wore a sheepskin waistcoat. Her head was partially covered by a white scarf that perched on top of her full, flowing hair.

Nikolai wanted to ask where he was, but his mind was too sluggish to put the words together. He shivered, although he was not cold. The girl smiled and put her arm around him. His mind raced. *Where am I? Who is this girl? I crash-landed up on the frozen lake. I did not dream that. Now I find myself here, lower down the Mountain, in the company of this strange girl.* He looked up at the young woman inquiringly. She smiled back at him reassuringly, but said nothing.

Nikolai made an attempt to get to his feet. It was a slow process. He felt dizzy, and his whole body ached. The girl responded by holding him steady while he regained his balance. *Maybe I am dreaming after all,* he thought. *Any minute I'll awaken to find myself still in the wreckage of the plane.* He ran his hands over his body. It was then that he realized that there was a long gash in his flying suit. It ran from his left shoulder down to his thigh. He could see his light blue overalls through the leather. Nikolai instinctively put his hand into the gash. There was no blood, but his side hurt. *Probably just bruised. I better check that later.* He surveyed the surrounding landscape. *I must be at least a thousand feet below the glacier.* He was in an alpine meadow, dotted with rocks that glistened in the morning sunlight. Just above this meadow, a track led up to a copse of juniper and beech.

"My name is Nikolai." He paused, and then he added, "But my friends call me Kolya. What's your name?"

The girl smiled but did not answer as she offered him her arm. Even if she had answered, Nikolai would not have heard, for in that same instant, darkness filled his mind, shutting down his thoughts. The light had gone. Nikolai collapsed, unconscious, into her outstretched arms.

Just before dawn, Nikolai awoke. As he opened his eyes he was partially aware that he was lying on a wooden pallet, over which a woolen blanket had been placed. He was covered with a sheepskin with a pillow made of coarse Hessian under his head. The blanket beneath him felt prickly to the touch. The first thing that came into focus was the figure of an old man sitting beside the pallet on a low stool. His head was bent, and he seemed to be counting under his breath. Nikolai attempted to sit up, but heaviness filled his body like lead, and he sank back on the pallet.

The old man looked up. Nikolai could see that he was holding a knotted woolen rope in his hands. His fingers were counting the knots as he looked at Nikolai. He smiled at the young man, but said nothing. Nikolai was struck by the beauty of the old man's face. Despite the ravages of time and exposure, the old man had a youthful appearance. There was not a single crease in his large, weather-tanned face. He wore a thick, white beard and long hair that was tied with a string that hung down his back. He was thick set with large, strong hands. *Am I dreaming again*, wondered Nikolai as he gazed at the figure watching over him.

The old man got up silently and went to a stove in the corner of the room. He returned with a bowl of steaming soup. "Come on, my lad. Get some of this down you," he said in perfect Russian.

Nikolai obediently opened his mouth as a crude wooden spoon was thrust to his lips.

The old man chuckled. "Yes, it's a bit on the warm side. But that's the best way to take it."

The soup was scalding hot, and yet Nikolai found he could swallow it all the same. He had never tasted anything like it. It reminded him of sour milk and pomegranates.

After a few minutes, the heaviness in his body began to disappear. He felt strength coming back to him and tried to sit up once more.

"Don't bother, for the moment," said the old man. "You'll be resting until the sun's up, and then you should be up on your feet."

Nikolai drifted back into sleep, only this time it was peaceful and deep.

The sun was high in the sky by the time he awoke again. He could see its glare from a tiny window. Although the room was dark, Nikolai could see that he was in a wooden cabin. He was lying in what he supposed was the main room. He looked around. The room contained the barest of furniture. There was a table under a tiny window and two chairs pushed up against it. There was the pallet on which Nikolai was lying and, in the opposite corner, a small cot covered with a nomad blanket woven from wool and goat hair. Above the cot was a spruce plank that served as a bookcase. It was piled with books in expensive bindings. They looked totally out of character in such primitive surroundings. The cabin smelled of a curious blend of olive oil, charcoal, and frankincense. The smells reminded Nikolai more of a church than a home.

In the far corner hung three oil lamps, their light illumining an assortment of icons, some painted and some simple oleograph prints. To his surprise he recognized an icon of Saint Nicholas the Wonderworker, his patron saint. He remembered his mother giving him a brass icon of his saint, but in the move to Aratsky, he had mislaid it. The saint looked at him accusingly.

Nikolai saw an old iron stove in another corner, and beside it, a samovar purred contentedly on a small table, its charcoal embers glowing in the dark. *This isn't real,* he thought *Have I gone back in time?*

As Nikolai was taking stock of his surroundings, a door in the back wall opened, and in walked the old man. Nikolai had not noticed this door before.

"Ah, I see you're awake. Well, that's good! There'll be a meal in half an hour. Can you get up?"

Nikolai sat up, swinging his legs gingerly onto the floor. He stood for a moment to get his balance and then slowly shuffled towards a chair the old man had offered him.

"I feel bruised all over."

"Well, that's the least of your worries. It's shock that's the killer."

"I can't believe I'm still alive."

"The saints be praised!" The old man patted Nikolai on the shoulder. His hand felt like a chunk of dense wood. Nikolai flinched. The old man laughed. "I know what you're thinking... but I do use an axe to chop wood." He chuckled again. "I got these hands through hard work. Yours are soft because you use your head instead."

Both men laughed out loud at this.

"Tonight we'll fix your aches and pains with mutton fat. But first, let's drink some tea."

# CHAPTER SIX

Nikolai did not relish the thought of being covered with sheep fat, but that was the least of his concerns. *What are more pressing are the questions that need to be answered. Who is this strange old man? Did he see that girl in the meadow? How am I going to get back to my squadron? Can I trust this man?* He needed answers, but he had a dread that he would not like them. Nikolai could not hold back his thoughts. His confused mind raced like a flywheel. "Where am I? And who are you?"

"Well, young man, you are in my cabin, and my name is Simeon." The old man busied himself with preparing the tea.

"But I don't understand." Nikolai paused. *Crashing on the Mountain was real enough, but nothing else makes any sense.* He looked about the room desperately. "Yes, but how did I get here?"

"My granddaughter found you. It's best not to ask questions until you have fully rested." Simeon began to pour tea from a blackened teapot into two glasses. He placed the glasses in silver-plated holders.

Nikolai was not happy with this answer either, but before he could protest or ask any more questions, the old man gently but firmly took his hand. Nikolai turned and met Simeon's eyes. The old man fixed him with a look that went deep inside Nikolai's troubled mind. The effect was like a healing balm that spread through his confusion and anxiety, leaving a calm fragrance that penetrated his whole body. But it was not to last for long, for when the old man brought two steaming glasses of tea and placed one on the table before Nikolai, his felt his anxiety return. He paused, fearful that the tea might be drugged. He sipped it cautiously, letting a mouthful of the golden liquid sit in his mouth, savoring it, and inhaling its delicious aroma at the same time. It spoke of summer and exotic blossoms. He felt the tea begin to lift his spirits. Both men sat in silence as they drank.

*Nikolai, do not give into your emotions,* he said to himself. *Keep calm and reason it out.* He turned to the old man. "You said your granddaughter found me?"

"Yes, in the meadow below our cabin."

"But how did I get there?"

"We do not know. But nothing happens by chance."

Nikolai shrugged. "I don't know what you mean."

"It means everything—every event in our lives is governed by Providence." Simeon stroked his beard and sighed. He turned to the icons in the corner, as if seeking confirmation. Then he turned to Nikolai. "Before we answer your questions, tell us about yourself, my young friend!"

Nikolai swallowed hard, trying to regain his composure. He had been briefed to give only his name and rank, should he be forced to land in enemy territory. This was enemy territory.

Simeon continued. "I can see by your fair hair and blues eyes that you are from the north."

"My name is Nikolai Andreevich Rostovksy. I am a lieutenant in the Imperial Air Force. My friends call me Kolya."

"Ah, Kolya," repeated the old man, smiling. "You didn't just drop out of the sky, did you?"

Nikolai ignored this question. He was not sure how much he should reveal. *Who is this old man? He is obviously a fellow Russian. But what is he doing here, on the wrong side of the Turkish border? And yet I suppose it would not hurt to explain how I came to be here, to give a brief but not detailed explanation.* Nikolai looked at Simeon. "As I said, I am a pilot in the Imperial Air Force. This is my first solo mission, or should I say, was my first." He paused, picking up his empty glass and turning it methodically in his hands. "But I bungled it."

"Did you deliberately crash your plane?"

"No! Of course not!"

"Then you didn't bungle it as you say. It bungled you." Simeon laughed. "And now we have an unexpected but welcome guest." He made the sign of the cross and continued. "Well, young Kolya, it was providence that brought you to us. Natasha found you lying in the meadow just below our cabin. How you got there in your state is a mystery." Simeon suddenly fell silent as if he was listening to something. He turned his face away from Nikolai and muttered something inaudible. Then, checking himself, he continued. "And some mysteries simply should not be delved into, at least not for the moment. The main thing, thank God, is that you are safe."

"I am very grateful to you both …" Nikolai felt relieved to have been rescued. He could have died of exposure up on the frozen lake. But what was even more frightening was to lose his sense of reality. Nothing made sense. For Nikolai the laws of physics were immutable; you simply didn't lose altitude like he had done. Neither did you crash-land on a frozen lake and wake up in a meadow. And what about that hangar he had seen? Was it real? It certainly seemed real at the time. "I need to get back to my squadron."

The old man refilled Nikolai's glass. "As soon as you get your strength back, we'll help you get back to your squadron."

"Thank you, but how? I'm downed in enemy territory and am at least 50 miles from base." Nikolai felt his hackles and the color in his face rising. "I don't see how you can possibly help. This is enemy territory."

"Enemy territory!" Simeon banged his hand on the table. "Wherever you live on Ararat, you're in some enemy's territory. Here it's the Turks. On the other side of the Mountain, it's the Kurds and Azeris. This whole area, including the great plain below, once belonged to the Kingdom of Armenia, and before that it was part of the Persian Empire. Kingdoms come and go, but man stays the same."

"I don't understand what that has to do with getting me back to my base. I still don't see how you can help, stuck up here in the middle of nowhere. I need to get back to my squadron somehow. It is vital that I report the movement of the Turkish army towards the Russian border." Nikolai was desperate. The old man did not seem to comprehend the seriousness of his situation or the importance of reporting the Turkish advance.

Totally ignoring the young pilot's rude response, Simeon continued, "It's a long haul, but we'll make sure that you get back, all the same." He smiled encouragingly at Nikolai. "But for the moment, you're not in a fit state to travel, at least not for a few days. Besides, it's a hazardous journey."

"But couldn't you send someone to warn my squadron?" Nikolai did not know what he meant by this. Who was there to send? It was a futile question.

"Makes very little difference now. If the Turks are on the move, they will be at the Aratsky Pass long before anyone from here could alert your army. It's a two day journey, at the least." The old man scratched his head and sighed. "You need to get your strength back before you attempt to set out across the Mountain. We'll send Kelim with you as a guide. It's something that old devil needs to do."

Nikolai stood up, leaning heavily on the table. "What about my wrecked plane?"

"There's nothing we can do about that. It's the Army's concern if they want to come and salvage the parts. But honestly, I don't think they'll risk sending a squadron of sappers into enemy territory to retrieve it."

Nikolai felt crushed by the enormity of his situation. He was behind enemy lines, with very little chance of getting back to base until he had at least gotten his strength back. And he only had the word of the old man that he would. *What if they are hiding their real feelings and are waiting for an opportunity to turn me over to the Turkish authorities? Surely it is not unusual for a grandfather and granddaughter to live a private and lonely life in a secluded area, but not on Ararat.*

The same unanswered questions tossed and turned in his mind. *How can these Russians be living here without approval of the Porte?* The crash, his wrecked plane, Turks approaching the border without warning, and the possibility of betrayal—all these fears welled up in his mind, ready to burst like the Mountain beneath his feet. Nikolai felt cornered. *Can I make a dash for it? No, that is not possible. I have not the strength to get beyond the cabin door. Once outside I would be at the mercy of the elements.* He sat down heavily on his chair. His head began to spin. The room went dark as a wave of adrenalin suddenly surged through his body. He almost fell off the chair as all his muscles went into spasm.

In a flash, the old man had rushed to his aid, supporting him with his strong arms. Nikolai began to tremble. There was no escape. He would have to trust Simeon and his granddaughter. All the same, he felt anger rising up in him. He blew through his teeth.

"But my plane can't just be left where it is!" hissed Nikolai in frustration.

"Well, you can't do anything about it."

"But it's too valuable to be left abandoned on the Mountain. What if the Turks find it?"

"The Turks don't come up here."

"How do you know that?"

"They're afraid of the Kurds."

"But you can't know for sure!"

"Nobody knows for sure. But it is unlikely," said Simeon. His voice was steady and void of any indignation at the young man's persistence.

"Well, you don't know. It's all conjecture." Nikolai paused. His anger was turning into dread. He had lost control of the SB-6, and now he was losing control of himself.

"My plane was personally designed and built by Sikorvsky," pleaded Nikolai.

"Well, the Kurds don't know that and will devour it all the same… if they haven't done so already."

"What do you mean 'devour'?"

"Our neighbors will pick over the bones in a matter of days. What they will do with the broken parts, I have no idea. I do know that they won't leave a scrap of evidence."

Nikolai was stunned by this information. His beloved SB-6 left for the picking over by local brigands. The latest Argus six cylinder being used for—who knows what by ignorant tribesmen. This was too much. "Nothing makes sense."

Simeon stared hard at the young man. "Nothing makes sense if you are so sure that nothing can exist outside of your own understanding."

"I don't know what you mean."

"It comes as a great shock to find yourself suddenly jolted out of what you consider to be reality and find yourself having to face a mystery."

"A mystery?"

"Yes, something that you cannot explain immediately."

"That does not answer my question." Nikolai glared at the old man. "I should have been killed when my aircraft plummeted in the mist, but it was caught up in a strange updraft." Nikolai's voice had an edge to it.

"Dragon's breath," said the old man.

"You know about Dragon's breath?"

"Yes. These fogs spring up year round, without warning. They are caused by hot puffs of gas from vents in the sides of the Mountain. The local people believe there is a dragon sleeping under the Mountain…."

Simeon smiled. "Well, they tell this to their children. They don't actually believe it. The story comes from the eruption in 1840, which blew out the side of the Mountain, carving out the Ahora Gorge."

"Still it doesn't explain how my plane was held in it. You don't fly over an area to find yourself back where you started!"

Simeon's face darkened. "Go on, my boy!"

"I must have been hallucinating," Nikolai continued. "You won't believe me, but I found an odd wooden structure, the size of a hangar, buried in the ice. I went inside…" He stopped, as if he had said enough already. He was choking on his words. "And then I don't remember anymore; except I had a strange dream, or I think it was a dream." His words trailed off in a whisper. He found himself sobbing as if he had lost everything in the world. He buried his head in his hands and let the tears flow.

The old man stood up and laid his hand gently on the young pilot's head. Then after going to the stove, he returned with a teapot. He poured the golden liquid into Nikolai's glass. "Come on, me boy. Drink some more tea!"

Nikolai did not hear the old man's words. He was lost once more in the confusion of his thoughts.

The old man laid his hand on Nikolai's head once more and whispered something under his breath. For a brief moment, the calm Nikolai had experienced earlier returned like a fleeting beam of sunlight in a darkened room.

Nikolai paused and looked up at Simeon. The old man had sat down beside him again. They sat for a few minutes in silence. The old man seemed lost in thought, as if he were in some other place. The calm had returned. Nikolai could not put into words what he felt at that time. But he was aware of an inner feeling of peace. No. It was more than that. It was a realization that his real self was buried somewhere deep within him. His anxiety, his fears were burdens that he carried around with him. They were real enough, but they were externals that could be laid aside like his flying suit. He did not have to wear them wherever he went. He felt an inner peace that he had never experienced in his life before. His tempestuous thoughts and anxiety had been silenced by something greater than he could possibly understand.

# CHAPTER SIX

"Go on Kolya,"

"Well, I had this dream. Or maybe I should say a nightmare. I dreamt someone was carrying me down the Mountain and gently set me down in the alpine meadow where your granddaughter found me. But... I'm not sure whether I dreamt it or not."

"You didn't dream it," said Simeon quietly. "It was Providence."

"Providence?"

"Yes, the hand of God."

Nikolai sank his head in his hands. Simeon spoke with an authority that could not be challenged. But Nikolai was not ready to simply accept what the old man said. He felt deep down that Simeon's words rang true, but he still had nagging doubts. *Am I going mad after all?* He knew that physics could not explain the miraculous landing or his arrival in the meadow. To his scientific mind and practical training, the very existence of these strange events was disturbing and too fantastic for words.

For Nikolai, there was no proof whatsoever of the existence of an omniscient force or what Simeon called Providence. He believed people believed whatever made their lives easiest. *If the old man and his granddaughter believe in God, that is fine. It's not that I don't believe, but it doesn't concern me personally.* And yet he had experienced, even if for just a brief moment, a realization that he could be wrong and that his real self, whatever that meant, was somehow buried in his image of himself.

*No! This is no good. There must be a rational explanation.* "Do you expect me to believe that? It's too bizarre for words." Nikolai's words were now a mixture of anger and fear.

"Well, until you can come up with a better explanation," replied Simeon calmly, "you had better be grateful for a spiritual solution."

"For that I am grateful." Nikolai's voice shook as he said this. *What is the old man getting at?*

"Well, Kolya, we need to eat. I am cooking a hare for lunch. It was only caught yesterday. It should make a fine meal." He looked at the stove, "And it's probably ready by now." The grandfather got up from his chair, went to the stove, and busied himself, stirring the stew with a large ladle. He lifted the ladle and took a sip. "Needs some more herbs." He took down a sprig of dried herb and careful added it to the pot.

Watching the old man about his daily chores suddenly made Nikolai feel ashamed of himself. "I want to thank you for rescuing me. I am very grateful, and I apologize for my outburst."

"I understand, my friend. Let's make further plans over a meal," Simeon said, returning with a tray on which three bowls of steaming stew and chunks of coarse rye bread were laid. "I'll call Natasha." The old man went and opened the door in the back wall. As Nikolai watched him, he saw that the door led into a cave behind the cabin. The old man called, and his granddaughter appeared in the doorway. It was the girl who had found him in the meadow. She smiled at Nikolai but said nothing.

"You get this down you, and you'll feel much better," Simeon said reassuringly.

The old man blessed the food, and the three of them tucked into a hearty meal.

Nikolai swallowed a mouthful of stew. "This is delicious."

"I'm glad you like it. We don't do too badly here on the Mountain," said the old man. "Tomorrow is another day."

Nikolai took some bread and dipped it in the stew. "Sufficient is the evil thereof," he replied, suddenly remembering this saying of his mother's.

After the meal, Nikolai asked if he could freshen up. His chin felt rough with two day's stubble, and there was dried blood on his hands and face. Simeon showed him a bowl and jug of water, which he had placed outside on the veranda. Natasha brought him a cake of soap and a linen towel. He splashed his face and hands in the cold mountain water. It made him wince for a brief second, but soon he felt a warm glow spread through his whole body. It felt good to wash his face and hands; although he had no means of shaving. He would have to be content with remaining unshaven until he got back to base. *I will look like a sailor—so what?* Nikolai ran his fingers through his hair in an attempt to tidy his appearance.

Instead of going back into the cabin, he decided to take a gentle stroll to test his legs. Outside he could smell the sweet odor of wood smoke. Its pale haze hung above a sod-covered roof that rudely jutted out from the jagged slabs of rock that rose up the steep side of the Mountain.

They looked like spikes on a dragon's back. Nikolai could see that the wooden cabin had been built into the entrance of a cave. Although its rough timbers were simply tree trunks, they had been skillfully fashioned to provide a substantial dwelling. The eaves of the roof provided covering for the open veranda that ran along the frontage. At one end of the cabin was a tiny door, hardly big enough to allow a full-grown man to enter. To the right of this elfin door was an equally small window with wooden shutters carved in the Novgorod style. The front of the cabin was festooned with lichen and moss, as were the giant rocks above the cave. This made the cabin blend into the surrounding terrain. *This is a secret place,* it seemed to say. It was totally invisible from the track below. *A whole army could pass by without noticing it,* thought Nikolai. He looked to the left of the cabin. There, the track ran along the edge of a steep ridge. It dropped away to a forest of junipers below.

Although his muscles ached, he was desperate to walk and get his body back to normal after his ordeal. The sun had broken through a watery mist that hung above the cabin. The air was sharp, and there was a strong smell of rotting pine needles and stagnant water that had collected in the pockets of rocks and the boles of the spruce. It felt good to be outside. Nikolai filled his lungs with the Mountain air. *I could probably manage a short stroll—anything to get my legs moving.*

As he set out, he found that the going was not as bad as he had feared. He maintained a steady pace along the track. Below he could see the great plain stretching for miles to the west. It was beginning to wear the brown and gray of the autumn swath. Immediately below, the terrain was covered with a dense carpet of oaks and acacia bushes, with an occasional outcrop of jagged rocks spiking the Mountain air like dragons' teeth. He had been thoroughly briefed not only in the topography of Ararat but also in its geology and history. If his bearings were correct, he would be heading towards the Ahora Gorge.

After walking for what seemed like half an hour, Nikolai came to a halt. He had reached the edge of a vast gorge. It fell away to the terrain below like a huge slice cut out of Ararat. He looked up. The mist was descending once more. He could just make out the tip of what he guessed was the Black Glacier with its slow-moving ice, melting endlessly into the Gorge. Where he was standing had once been a village. On the opposite side of the Gorge, an Armenian monastery containing a piece of the ark had once stood. All this had been swept away by the displeasure of the Mountain over seventy-six years ago.

A slice had been hacked out of Nikolai's reality too. Nikolai sat down on a rock to think. Foremost in his mind was the thought of getting back to his squadron. He knew the journey would be difficult and dangerous, but he could not stay where he was. His SB-6 was a write-off. He had no wish to go back to the wreckage. Even if he could have salvaged some parts, he would not be able to carry them across the Mountain. And he would have to cross the Mountain. To follow the tracks below would mean certain capture. There was no alternative but to wait and see what Simeon would come up with.

Nikolai decided to make his way back to the cabin. The sun was setting. It would soon be dusk. He was fully aware that this was the time that predators began the hunt.

He had learned that when he hunted with fellow officers in the Caucuses. It was not safe to be alone out on the Mountain.

On his way back, Nikolai had to pass a stretch of dense spruce and juniper that covered the slope above and below the track. He had not taken much notice of the wood in daylight, but now, in the early dusk, it appeared dark and menacing. As he walked he was aware of movement in the wood below. It was shadow-like and silent. And whatever it was, it was moving parallel to the track. Nikolai had avidly read the journals of the explorer Parrott who related how he had been stalked on several occasions by wolves and bears. Once he had been followed by a mountain lion. Nikolai quickened his pace. He was still not in good enough physical shape to be able to run, but he hurried as best he could. Should anything decide to spring out, it would find him easy prey.

Then he saw it. As he hurried around a sharp bend of the track, the trees thinned out into a glade, and it came bounding up the slope and onto the track in front of him. Nikolai was standing face to face with a large, gray wolf. The creature glanced at him, sniffed the air, and then broke out into a trot along the track towards the cabin. Nikolai blew through his teeth. *That was a close shave.* He waited for a few seconds, then when he was sure that the wolf was out of sight, he followed slowly and cautiously. Several yards down the track Nikolai stopped again. *Is my mind playing tricks?* The scene before him was straight out of a fairy tale. Just a few yards away, he caught sight of Natasha. She was sitting on a fallen spruce just below the track. Beside her sat the gray wolf with its huge head on her lap. She was stroking its ears as if it were a domestic dog.

As Nikolai approached, the wolf looked up and sprang to its feet. It sniffed the air and then slunk silently into a dense growth of small oaks. Natasha looked up and smiled. Then she lifted her hand in warning. *Do not approach,* her eyes said. Nikolai paused and then saw the need for caution. No sooner had the wolf disappeared into the wood than another wild animal appeared. Nikolai could not believe his eyes. To Natasha's left, a little below where she was sitting, the enormous head of a black bear appeared. It looked around and, like the wolf, sniffed the air. Then its full form emerged from the trees. Nikolai had seen bears in the Caucasus, but never as big as this creature that was trundling towards Natasha. The bear came right up to her and sniffed her hands. Natasha reached into a cloth bag that lay on the rocks beside her. She produced a hunk of dried bread. The great beast took the bread gently in its mouth and stood before her chewing it, with what seemed to Nikolai to be great pleasure. Like the wolf previously, the huge bear turned and sniffed the air once more and ambled slowly into the darkness of the trees.

Natasha stood up and beckoned to Nikolai. *Am I dreaming? Is she really standing there?* Nikolai walked towards Natasha and reached out his hand to touch her arm, half expecting her to disappear in a wave of magic. But the fairy princess was real enough. She stood there firm and human. Natasha smiled at Nikolai and took his arm. "Weren't you afraid?" stammered Nikolai. "Why did they not harm you?" His questions sounded foolish. Natasha did not answer but led Nikolai in silence along the track to the cabin. He did not ask any more questions. He knew that this was her personal secret, to be shared only with the Mountain.

Just before they reached the cabin, Natasha turned off quickly and disappeared into the dark of a patch of junipers. Nikolai did not follow her. *What is she up to now? Maybe she is visiting a sick owl.*

# CHAPTER SEVEN

THE VISIBILITY THE following morning proved to be too poor for the patrol to renew the ascent of the Mountain that day. A cold fog hung in the air in thick patches immediately above their encampment. Even below the mist, the air was cold and damp. The men shivered as they emerged from their goatskin shelters. As if mocking their predicament, the twin peaks of Ararat glistened defiantly in the morning sun.

*Forbidden for some,* Ahmet Ali thought as he looked up at the Mountain. "But not for us this time," he said aloud to himself as he adjusted the saddle on his horse.

Javad and Vugor joined him.

"We can't climb this morning. We have to wait until the fog lifts."

"It looks to me that it won't lift," said Javad.

Vugor shook his head in agreement. "Yes. He's right, Offendi."

"Well, in that case, we shall wait," Ahmet Ali replied sourly.

They did not resume their search for the plane for two days. It was on the third day that the patrol set out at first light. They thought they would have two to three hours of clear weather, although this was not guaranteed. The character of the Mountain could change suddenly, without warning. Javad led the patrol, followed by the captain, with Vugor bringing up the rear. The patrol was reduced to eleven men. Those who were too afraid to continue had been dismissed. The captain had decided that their services would not be needed in the future—mercenaries were plentiful, so they would not be missed.

By mid-morning they had reached their former encampment and dismounted. Everything appeared calm. In broad daylight the previous experience on the Mountain seemed distant and unreal. Besides, the men were too busy fixing their rifles and backpacks to worry about invisible spirits. Their main concern was running into a visible band of Kurds.

Javad went on ahead with Vugor. The terrain consisted of countless boulders of all shapes and sizes, covered with emerald and gold lichen—an ideal scenario for an ambush. If there were any Mountain Kurds hiding among the rocks, Javad and Vugor would spot them. They did not need eyes for this purpose.

It was his hunter's instinct that stopped Javad suddenly in his tracks. He was conscious of something moving to the right of the track. He quickly dropped on all fours and pressed his ear to the ground. There was nothing to be heard. Vugor, alert as always, had followed suit. He lay beside Javad, fingering the trigger of his rifle. Javad sat up and looked at Vugor. He nodded his head and pointed to a clump of acacia immediately to their right. Not a sound passed between them. *Nothing to be seen, nothing to be heard, but there is a presence all the same.*

Slowly Javad got to his feet, signaled silently to Vugor, and set off briskly back down the track with his fellow scout following. From time to time Vugor looked back. But there was nothing to be seen. *Perhaps Javad imagined it*, he thought. But he knew that his brother Azeri was never wrong in these matters. It was not until they reached the camp that Vugor spoke, "What was it?"

"I'm not sure."

"It was probably a bear?"

"It didn't move like a bear."

"But how can you be sure. You didn't see it."

Javad looked hard at the other scout. "I sensed it. It was real."

Javad went to find the captain. Once he did, he reported his encounter.

"But you say you didn't see anything?" asked the captain.

"I felt it, Offendi." replied Javad.

Vugor nodded in assent. He had not heard or seen anything, but he knew from experience that Javad had.

"Do you think the Kurds have spotted us?" The captain rested his hand on his holster.

"I don't think so." Javad automatically cocked his Mauser. "The Kurds are not subtle. They just attack."

"It was probably an animal. Possibly a bear or mountain lion," added Vugor.

Javad looked doubtful but said nothing.

"Well, whatever it was, we need to push on." The captain straightened his tunic. "I think you had better stay with us. We need to keep together. I don't want you picked off by an ambush."

The patrol resumed its trek up the Mountain. The climb was becoming more difficult. In some places it was so steep they had to pull themselves up on the rocks that protruded at intervals in the narrow track. Scrambling in this fashion for what seemed hours, they came to a flat, narrow plateau that stretched along the edge of the Mountain.

The men stopped to get their breath and to survey the area. Ahmet Ali pulled out a pair of binoculars from his backpack. He made a panoramic sweep of the plateau and of the climb that lay ahead of them on the far side of the plateau. As he did this, he paused and refocused the binoculars on a particular spot. It looked like smoke. It hovered over a ridge just west of the Ahora Gorge. He quickly offered the binoculars to Javad. "Is that smoke or a wisp of cloud?"

Javad pointed the binoculars in the direction indicated by the captain. "Smoke!"

"Must be a Kurd encampment," said Vugor.

"Maybe not. It's probably a nomad camp." The Captain returned the binoculars to his backpack. "Let's go around it, just the same. I would rather we keep clear of them for the moment. I don't want to bring attention to ourselves and get involved in an unnecessary skirmish."

"Very wise, Offendi," replied Javad. "Walking into a nomad camp would be asking for a bullet through the head."

Ahmet Ali ordered the men to keep low and watchful. "We'll climb above the spot where the smoke is and, if necessary, attack them from above. But better to leave well enough alone."

Ahmet Ali looked up. By the position of the sun, the patrol had exceeded not only the two hours but the three hours too. However there was no change in the weather. The mountain appeared exceptionally calm and peaceful. Crossing the level ground of the plateau allowed them to regain their strength. On reaching the edge of the plateau they were forced to climb almost vertically once more. The track was now wider which made it more difficult. There were no rocks to hold onto. The men cursed as they slipped on loose stones. After a while the track narrowed once more, allowing the men to grasp its stony sides for support.

They were now climbing steadily upwards into the sun. There were fewer trees; only the deep-rooted and strongest survived here. They grew from splits in the rock, their bulging roots providing handholds. Although this made the going easier, the track had become slippery. Ahmet Ali knew that they were nearing the snowline. Run-offs from the glacier trickled down the center of the trail. If the men noticed this, they would realize that they had already climbed higher than they'd intended. Javad and Vugor obviously knew this, but said nothing. *So far so good,* thought the captain. *At this rate we should reach the glacier before the sun sinks.*

After another hour of almost vertical climbing, the terrain leveled out. They were now above the tree line. Patches of snow lay among the solitary rocks. Ahmet Ali realized that he had brought his men farther than they had been willing to go. Perhaps he could spur them on to the glacier, where he was certain the Russian plane had crashed. He stopped and turned to Javad. "Let's rest here for the moment."

As they rested, Ahmet Ali was disturbed by a nagging thought that the smoke on the ridge was not from a nomad's camp. At first he had assumed that it was, but now he was not so sure. *Could it have been from a fire lit by a downed pilot?* He had to know. The captain summoned Javad. "That was smoke we saw?"

"Yes, of course, Offendi."

"Probably from a nomad's camp?"

"I don't see what else it could be," replied Javad, examining the captain with curiosity.

"Well, I am not convinced."

"What else could it be?"

"A downed pilot."

Javad did not reply. He looked at the captain and then nodded. "I see what you mean."

"If it is, then I need to investigate."

"And if it isn't?"

"I'm not planning to go barging into that hornets' nest and end up with a bullet in my brain. I am not looking for a skirmish with the nomads. No, this requires stealth. I will simply reconnoiter." Ahmet Ali paused and fingered his revolver. "But if it is what I suspect," the captain had a gut feeling that he would find the pilot, "then I will do what is necessary."

"Do you want me to go with you, Offendi?"

"No. I want you to head the patrol. I'll take five men. That should be sufficient. But I want you to select them."

"Yes, Offendi." Javad saluted in his sloppy fashion and went to rouse suitable men for the task.

# CHAPTER EIGHT

THE SUN HAD sunk behind the Mountain by the time Nikolai returned to the cabin. He kept wondering, *where did Natasha go? Why did she not speak to me?*

Entering the cabin, Nikolai saw that the samovar had been placed on the table. He could hear the water just coming to the boil.

"Ah, you're back. Just in time for supper," said Simeon. "Have you seen Natasha?"

"I met her down the track, but she went off somewhere else." Nikolai felt stupid trying to explain what had happened. The strange girl had ignored his questions and had walked off into the woods.

"Ah, well, it's time to light the lamps. But first, let's pray." The old man went and fetched an old, worn prayer book. Its pages were blackened at the edges from years of being handled by oily and charcoaled fingers.

Nikolai did not understand the prayers. Simeon read them in the Old Church Slavonic. Nikolai did however recognize the Lord's Prayer, although he was at a loss to repeat it himself. He felt embarrassed, as if he had intruded into the private lives of the old man and his granddaughter. This was an intimate time, when they prayed before the icons in the glow of the oil lamps that hung before them. He felt awkward. He had no time for church, or any kind of religion for that matter. Now here he was, forced to eavesdrop on the private devotion of these simple people. For all his knowledge of aeronautical science—he had been a brilliant student—he felt totally out of his element standing with the grandfather in prayer.

After the old man finished reading the prayers, he lit an oil lamp, which he placed at the center of the table. He then went to the stove and busied himself, making soup for their supper. Nikolai sat at the table and waited.

The door to the cabin opened, and Natasha came in. Her hands were cupped, and Nikolai noticed that something was fluttering between her fingers. Nikolai looked at her in surprise. Natasha came and sat down next to him at the table. She opened her hands. There, sitting within, was a tiny bird. It stretched its wings and idly pecked at Natasha's fingers. She, in turn, gently caressed its wings. The tiny creature sat there as if it were at home. Then Natasha stood up and went to the door of the cabin. She opened it with one hand, and then with the other, she gently tossed the tiny bird into the air. It sped away like a bullet, disappearing into the dusk. She stood for a moment, gazing after the bird. Then she turned and smiled at Nikolai. And then, as if suddenly remembering something, she crossed the room and disappeared through the door into the cave at the back of the cabin.

If Simeon had noticed this strange encounter with the bird, he did not show it. Instead, he turned to Nikolai and said, "Soup will be ready soon." A savory smell of wild herbs wafted through the room from the contents of an old, black pot on the stove.

"Natasha should be back soon," he said, coming to the table. "And then we can eat."

Nikolai looked up at Simeon enquiringly. *What next?*

The old man pulled up a chair and sat opposite Nikolai. He studied the young man's face for a few moments and then began to speak in a low tone. "You're probably wondering how we got here. Yes, I know, it does seem strange—but there is an explanation for everything….even if it does not fit easily into our perception of reality."

Simeon glanced at the door that led into the cave for a moment and then continued. "I was a soldier in the war against Turkey, serving under Lieutenant-General Ter-Ghukasov. He was of Armenian descent, and I must say, a brilliant commander. It was the forces under Ter-Ghukasov, stationed near Yerevan, which began the first assault into

Ottoman territory by capturing the town of Bayazid." The old man paused to think. "Yes, it was on the 27th of April, 1877. Capitalizing on Ter-Ghukasov's victory in Bayazid, our forces advanced further, taking the region of Ardahan on the 17th of May. The Russian Infantry unit in which I served also besieged the region of Kars in the final week of May, although Turkish reinforcements lifted the siege and repulsed us. There was fierce fighting all around. We were a small detachment, and in the heat of battle, we became separated from the main Russian army. We were also poorly equipped and soon ran out of ammunition. It was only a matter of time before the Turks realized this. We were forced to surrender. I can tell you, I didn't like the idea of being a prisoner of war. But what could we do?

We were herded into a makeshift camp and addressed by a Turkish officer who spoke some Russian. It appeared that we were to be ransomed. If that failed, we would be sold as slaves. Yes, slavery was still rife in this area, even at that time." Simeon crossed himself. "My comrade Guram and I decided to escape. We prayed like we have never prayed before, and the following night, we decided to make a break for it. It was a cloudy night as we crept to the outer perimeter of the camp. Usually two soldiers patrolled, approaching each other from different parts of the perimeter. This night, there was no one to be seen. We waited, hoping that the guards would pass by, and then we would make a dash for it. If they did not shoot us, they would probably hunt us down easily, but that was the risk we would take. We waited for what seemed hours, but no one came. We could not believe our luck. No guards, or were they hiding in ambush? It did not seem likely. Well, we made a dash for it. We sped out of the camp like hares. We ran and ran for at least an hour. There was no sign of pursuit, and after two days, we arrived at the Russian frontier. There, my comrade and I separated. Guram, who was a mercenary, went home to his native Yerevan, and I went north to find my regiment."

Nikolai leaned back in his chair, shaking his head in silent wonder at the old man's story.

Simeon continued. "After many adventures, I finally rejoined my regiment. I reported what had happened and heard no more. A few months later, I was discharged from the Army and set out for my home in a village near Simferopol. My plan was to take leave of my family and then set out for Mount Athos. My platoon commander, Ptichkin, had already gone to the Holy Mountain to become a monk. I wanted to do the same. I had been greatly impressed by him. He was a remarkable man, much loved by the men. He was never without his pipe, whether alight or not. He was like a father to us. Although he was of good breeding, he nevertheless refused to speak French, preferring to speak his native Russian. He also shunned society and spent his spare time reading the Bible and other spiritual books. Ptichkin was awarded the highest honor by the Sovereign himself and was offered a prestigious position in the War Office, but he declined it, and went off to some monastery on Mount Athos. I would like to have followed him to the monastery, but my destiny was to be different.

On returning to my village after demobilization, I found that cholera had taken my family and friends. I had a daughter living in Omsk, and so I sought her out. The journey was a long, arduous affair, but I made it, only to be stopped on the outskirts of the city by militia. They told me that the area had been quarantined, and that if I entered the city, I would not be able to leave again. Cholera had struck there, too.

I decided to risk it and enter the city. As I walked down a myriad of empty streets, I came across an old woman sitting, barefooted on the steps of an old, wooden church. I asked her if she knew the whereabouts of my daughter. My daughter had married a Frenchman, and in a town like this, she would be known as the lady who married a foreigner. The old woman was silent at first and then pointed at a house a few yards beyond the church.

I thanked her and approached the house. There was an uncanny silence, as if everyone was asleep. As I entered the porch, I realized that cholera had claimed my daughter and her husband too. Their bodies lay crumpled in the hallway. Their faces had turned black, and there was sickly smell of death in the air. Turning to go, I suddenly caught sight of a little girl sitting on the stairs. She was alive, but her eyes were dull and vacant. She sat silently, staring fixedly at something that was not there. She didn't cry or make any sound. Without thinking, I scooped her up in my arms. It was a dangerous thing to do with all that cholera around. But she was my granddaughter; what else could I do?

Well, God was with me. Neither of us caught cholera, and just as I had passed through the Turkish lines, I passed unnoticed through the cordon set up by the militia.

Once we were away from Omsk, I took stock of the situation. I could not abandon her and go off to the Holy Mountain, so instead, I decided to make a pilgrimage of the holy places of Russia and take her with me. I hoped to find a miraculous cure for my granddaughter. But despite praying at the shrines of the saints, she never recovered her voice. The effects of shock have remained to this day."

"So that's why she did not answer me!" Nikolai paused. "Has she never spoken?"

"Not in words."

"But how do you communicate with each other?"

"She understands speech, and I understand her body language and facial expressions. It suffices."

"But she has a very intelligent face. Can she read and write, or is that a stupid question?"

"Yes, she can read. Most of the books you see in the cabin, I bought for her. She is an avid reader and very knowledgeable. When she wants to, she sometimes writes on a wax tablet I made for her." Simeon paused and looked at his hands.

"Please go on with your story."

"As I could not carry out my wish to go to the Holy Mountain of Athos, I decided to come here to the Holy Mountain of Noah. That did not happen immediately, of course. In fact, we were on the road for five years, visiting monasteries and churches and meeting with all kinds of healers and people of prayer. By this time, Natasha was thirteen years old. I decided to leave her with a family in Simferopol, but she did not want to leave me. I had set my heart on the life of a hermit, somewhere away from people." Simeon crossed himself and sighed. "I chose Ararat since I had been a prisoner of war in this region. During the brief period in the camp, I could see the splendor of the Mountain every day. I must have known even then that my destiny lay on its slopes. For as formidable and desolate as it appeared, its spiritual history and beauty attracted me greatly.

To be brief, I decided to set out for Mount Ararat and take Natasha with me. I know it sounds irresponsible, but as soon as we reached the

Turkish border, I knew instinctively that this was God's will. Trusting in Providence, I dressed Natasha as a boy, and I put on my old military greatcoat, complete with my campaign ribbon from the Russian-Ottoman war of 1878. I didn't see any reason to remove them, and we crossed the border into Turkish territory near Erzurum.

At the frontier, we were stopped by a captain of the Turkish gendarmerie, who, seeing the ribbon, saluted me and politely offered me some coffee and liqueur. I had never tasted such things before, and so I declined. The officer wrote a letter and gave it to me.

Just near the Aratsky Pass, we were stopped again. This time we were arrested by a young lieutenant and taken before his commanding officer. After showing him my letter from the captain of gendarmerie, we were allowed to continue. To this day I do not know what it said. It was written in Arabic script. I still have it. I only had to show it once more, on the last leg of our journey, and it worked wonders. Finally, we came here, and with help of the local nomads built this cabin in the mouth of the cave."

"I don't understand how you managed to pass the Turkish checkpoints. Surely they would not welcome a Russian soldier?"

"But they did. I learned later that they had great respect for Russian soldiers."

"But, why?"

"We were fierce fighters, and so I suppose the Turks regarded us as worthy opponents."

"But how did you manage to get help from the nomads?"

"That was the work of Providence, too." Simeon adopted an even quieter tone. "You see, I knew in my heart that God was calling me to Ararat. I knew it was against all reason and that I was putting my granddaughter at great risk. But there are occasions when you have to do what you have to do." The old man smiled. "The local nomads consider this mountain to be a holy place. When we arrived, as it were, out of the blue, they could not understand how we had gotten here. Rumor spread that I was descended from Nuh, whom we call Noah, and that God had sent me to reclaim the ark."

Nikolai's eyes bulged in amazement. "You don't mean Noah in the Bible, do you?"

"The same. The local tribes believe the Mountain of Nuh cannot be climbed, except by a descendant of Noah. They believe that the ark of Noah is near the top of the Mountain, and it will stay there out of reach of man because it is the command of Allah."

"They just accepted you as this...descendant?"

"Well, there is more to it than that...." Simeon paused. The door to the cave opened, and Natasha entered the room. Without stopping to communicate anything to her grandfather, she crossed the room and went outside.

"But I don't understand," Nikolai said, watching her leave. "What does your granddaughter do all day?"

"If you are thinking that this is no place for a young girl, then I do not agree."

"But she can't live here forever, can she?"

"If she wants to. But I think you mean what will happen when I die."

Nikolai's face reddened. "Well, you won't live forever."

"Not here, my boy. That's true." He stroked his beard thoughtfully and then stood up.

Meanwhile, Natasha reappeared. She was carrying a basket of dried bread, which she placed next to the stove. She then began to arrange bowls for their supper.

"You go ahead and serve the stew. We'll be back in a moment."

Natasha stopped what she was doing and came and kissed her grandfather on the cheek.

The old man laughed and turned to Nikolai. "Come on, Kolya. I want to show you something." Simeon went to the door at the back of the cabin, opened it, and beckoned Nikolai to follow him.

The door opened into the cave behind the cabin. Inside, an oil lamp flickered, casting long shadows on the limestone walls. The ceiling was too high to be visible, and Nikolai wondered how far back the cave went inside the Mountain.

"Yes, it's quite impressive," said Simeon in response to Nikolai's expression of wonder. "It probably extends for miles. There are numerous tunnels branching from this cave, going off to only God knows where. I blocked up my part to keep out wandering bears, wolves, and other unwanted visitors!" Simeon took up a small candle lantern from a shelf fixed to the wall and lit it. "I use the cave for storage. It's remarkably dry, and I can store bread here for months." He stepped forward into the gloom. "Come on. That is not what I want to show you."

They went further into the cave, until they came to a great wall of rocks that had obviously been piled up to seal off the cave from wild animals and intruders. To the left of the wall, a deep trench had been dug. There was a pile of smaller rocks stacked beside it. "You asked about the future? Well, when it is time for me to depart this earth, I have requested that Natasha lay my body here," Simeon said, pointing at the trench. "This is my grave."

Nikolai did not know what to say. He knew that people bought burial plots in preparation for their death, and of course, he was familiar with family vaults, which were very popular in St. Petersburg. But he had never been shown one, nor had he ever considered such morbid arrangements. He was young. Death was far away. It did not concern him.

"We cannot avoid the inevitable," Simeon said, as if reading Nikolai's thoughts. "You should know, being a pilot."

These words hit Nikolai like lightning. They suddenly awoke the memory of Andriadi. *I was fortunate to have the best instructor in the Air Force,* he mused. *God rest his soul! I owe everything to you, dear Ivan Ivanovich.* Captain Ivan Ivanovich Andriadi's career as an aviator was as brilliant as it was tragically short. Nikolai's mentor had not had time to think about his end. Simeon's preoccupation with death had triggered a mental block in Nikolai's mind. It was the same when anything bordered on the supernatural. Nikolai felt confused. "I need some fresh air," he said, trying to change the subject.

"Yes. The air in here is not too good. Well, you go and breathe some of our mountain air, and then we'll have supper."

As Nikolai reached the door to the cabin, Simeon called out, "Remember the soup's ready!"

"I am just going to step outside for a moment. I am not planning to go anywhere."

The old man nodded and blew out the lantern. Nikolai opened the main door to the cabin and took several deep long breaths.

# CHAPTER NINE

**N**IKOLAI AWOKE JUST before dawn, while it was still dark outside. Simeon was busy preparing something on the stove. Nikolai sat on the edge of the bed and stretched.

"Ah, I see you're awake," said the old man. "How do you feel?"

"Quite normal. Thank you." Nikolai felt much better, especially after Simeon had smothered his arms, chest, and legs with mutton fat. The smell was unbearable, but his body had stopped aching, and he felt his strength gradually beginning to return. Although his legs were still bruised, they did not hurt. His hands bore marks of discoloration, but there was no pain.

"You seemed to have recovered much sooner than I expected. Well, you're young and healthy, so your body quickly repairs itself."

"Thanks to your care." Nikolai got up and slid into his flying overalls. Having put on his leather boots, he went over to Simeon. They embraced, and Simeon indicated a place at the table.

"Sit down, Kolya, and I'll bring you some tea."

"Simeon?"

"Yes?"

"Is there anything I can do to help? I can't just sit around and watch you. I would like to at least make some contribution for your hospitality"

"You, my boy, need this time to recoup your strength. Anyway, we are pleased to have a guest. Do some walking. You are no extra burden, if you are thinking that. Besides, you need to think about your future."

Simeon had again said something that Nikolai did not understand. It was not just the words; there seemed to be a much deeper meaning when the old man spoke. Nikolai shook his head and said, "Well, if you are sure, then I would like to climb up to the glacier today."

"Well, I think you're fit enough, but there are other things to consider."

"Like what?"

"The climb is not difficult, but there can be unexpected hazards."

"Hazards?"

"Yes, on the upper slopes there are often lightning strikes and the occasional volcanic bomb."

"Bomb! Did you say bomb?"

"Yes. It has been known for large boulders to work loose and come crashing down the Mountain at high speed and without any warning."

Nikolai shook his head in disbelief.

"Kelim, for example, was struck by lightning and lived to tell the tale."

"Who is Kelim?"

"He is a nomad chief. He was pinned for several minutes to a rock. He said it was like having long skewers stuck through his body—like a roasting lamb. His rifle became a molten mess, and the brass buckle on his belt melted. He told me that the lightning was attracted to anything metal. His favorite cooking pot melted too."

"There is a buildup of electricity in the low cloud, I suppose," said Nikolai. "And then it discharges itself as lightning. But I don't understand the bombs—how can they happen without warning?"

"I saw one myself when I was visiting the nomads on the eastern slope. It came hurtling down the Mountain like a demon. It was big enough to crush a man." Simeon crossed himself. "By the grace of God, I managed to dash to safety –just in time. I did not see it coming, but I heard it." He looked at Nikolai with great concern. "There are wild animals too, but with God's help and prayer, you should be safe from them."

"What kind of animals?"

"Bears, mountain lions, and wolves."

"But how do they manage to live up here in this desolate region?"

"The area abounds in deep caves, tunnels, and nooks and crannies carved into the limestone. These are the homes not only of the carnivores but also of poisonous snakes, on the lower slopes, that is."

"Is this cave one of them?" asked Nikolai in alarm.

"It was," Simeon laughed. "But when we moved in, the serpents moved out. They did not wish to cohabit with us Russians!"

"And what about the nomads? I have heard that the Kurds are pretty fierce and don't like strangers."

"It's true. You probably mean the Hasasori Nomads. They are accomplished fighters. Their reputation keeps unwanted visitors at bay. They are very jealous of their way of life, guarding it zealously from outsiders, and in general, shunning any outside influence. There are other Kurds besides the Hasasori, but they don't live on the Mountain. They only hunt on the lower slopes."

"Yet, the Hasasori accepted you and your granddaughter."

"God knows why." Simeon said, crossing himself.

"Where do they live?"

"They live higher up the Mountain, on the yavala."

"The yavala?"

"Yes, it's a plateau where their sheep graze. At the first signs of winter, they abandon the plateau and move their camp to the lower slopes of the Mountain. They are the guardians of this biblical mountain, protecting it from infidels who are bold enough to set foot on this holy place."

"Do they speak Russian?" "Some do. But it is very limited. Their language is Kurmanji." Simeon sighed.

"They are good, simple people. They will not bother you, since you are our guest. Besides, I sent Natasha this morning to seek help for your journey back to your regiment. You could not make the journey without an experienced guide."

"But isn't Natasha at risk?" Nikolai suddenly felt concern for her.

"Not with the Kurds, and besides, Saint Nikolai will accompany her on the climb."

Nikolai was not consoled by this answer. *If there are lightning storms and volcanic bombs, apart from wild beasts, how could a young girl fare alone on the Mountain?* Simeon's apparent complacency bothered him. "I can't believe you let her go alone."

"Natasha can take care of herself," Simeon said quietly. "She knows every inch of the Mountain."

Nikolai shook his head in disbelief. "When did she set out?"

"Not long ago. If you set out now you could catch up to her before she makes for the nomad camp."

Nikolai jumped to his feet, gulping down his glass of tea and placing the glass on the table. "I'll go at once!" He picked up his pilot's scarf and wrapped it around his neck.

"Well, you'll need to take the first track west of the cabin. It's a bit steep at first, but you'll gain time, and after a while, it levels out." Simeon took a sheepskin waistcoat off a peg on the door. "And you'll need this for the journey." He turned and picked up a felt cap that lay on one of the chairs. "And take this felt cap too. It's going to be colder higher up, despite the brilliant sunshine of the day." He then went over to the stove and filled a bag with a supply of cheese and dry bread, which he offered to Nikolai.

Nikolai took the bag and swung it over his shoulder. "Thank you. Forgive my rudeness. I have a lot to learn."

Simeon smiled and patted Nikolai on the shoulder. "God go with you, Kolya!"

Nikolai opened the door to the cabin and strode off into the darkness of the early morning. Simeon stood at the door and made the sign of the cross over Nikolai's departing figure.

Nikolai found the track easily. At a glance, the track up the rock face looked too steep. However, as he climbed, he found that it was not as difficult as it appeared. It was hard going at first, but Nikolai's desire to meet up with Natasha gave him a special energy. He felt the adrenaline surging through his body as he climbed determinedly up the rocky track.

By his reckoning, he decided this was probably the best way up to the glacier. *Probably a five hour climb.* Already the dawn was breaking over the landscape, and after an hour's steady climb, the sun was bright in a blue sky. There was no hint of mist, although Simeon had cautioned him that the weather could change abruptly, in a matter of minutes.

Simeon had told him not to venture off the path, and should he be caught in the clouds, to remain where he was until they lifted. Under no circumstances was he to forget this. He should also keep a lookout for bears and mountain lions at this altitude, and keep clear of them.

Nikolai laughed to himself. *Keep on the track indeed! What if I meet a bear or lion? There's nowhere to go.* The track wound its way through a dense mat of thorns and impenetrable bushes, spiked here and there by sharp rocks. Although the upper parts of the track were merely yards away at times, even a lion would find it impossible to leave the track in pursuit.

Nikolai checked the position of the sun to determine the time. He calculated that it was around nine in the morning. Above his head, gigantic, rocky peaks soared almost straight up. Nikolai climbed now with ease. The air was crisp. The track headed east and disappeared around a huge, yellow-lichen-covered rock, the size of an airship. As he rounded the giant rock, he stopped in amazement. To his right the steep track leveled into an alpine meadow. It came as a complete surprise for him to find an open, grassy place amidst the barren rocks and crags of this part of the Mountain. As he stepped into the meadow, he realized that what he had taken for grass was in fact small bushes that covered the ground like a carpet. Amidst this green were the most beautiful flowers he had ever seen. There were white and yellow blossoms and delicate, blood red, thorn-like plants that seem to pierce the alpine air. There was a carpet of purple saxifrage that ran through the center of the meadow. At the edge of the meadow, there were pink flowers that grew in densely tufted clusters among the smaller rocks. The clusters formed domed cushions, with long shoots supporting delicate petals. There were other purples and blues everywhere.

Nikolai felt awkward and clumsy, treading on this wondrous carpet of nature. But he knew that whether he intruded here or not, this remote pocket of natural beauty would inevitably disappear, smothered under the heavy blizzards of winter or the rockslides of the restless mountain. These exquisite plants would die, mown down by rock and ice, and next spring, their offspring would emerge and stand tall and defiant….But today, the meadow basked in the brilliant autumn sun.

Nikolai sat and rested on a rock, listening to the voice of the Mountain. A gentle breeze stirred the flowers, and a skylark trilled overhead. The incessant buzzing of insect wings provided a gentle ostinato.

From time to time he could hear the plaintive cry of wheatears, sitting high on their stony perches, from which they watched him warily. *Why does such beauty hide itself away on the bleak and dangerous slopes of Ararat—high up, out of the reach of travelers, only to be discovered by the occasional nomad or climber? Why did such loveliness grow here where no one could see it? Who planted this harmonious Eden amidst the chaos and turmoil of the Mountain?*

*Natasha. She too is like one of these alpine flowers, a precious jewel, hidden away up here in the remoteness of the Mountain.* But Nikolai had found her. His life was not to be the same any more. He gently plucked a delicate blossom and placed it in his shirt pocket.

As Simeon had told him, this was the forbidden mountain, the home to snakes, scorpions, bears, and man-eating wolves. Simeon had told him that pilgrims had climbed Ararat in search of the legendary ark. *Perhaps they also visited this beautiful oasis on the Mountain. Perhaps the blood-red thorns sprang up from the graves of saintly pilgrims who reposed on the hazardous journey, and this meadow is their memorial.*

Up here, Nikolai felt at ease, as he had for a brief moment when talking with Simeon. Here he could think clearly. He could think about such things as never before. In his logical mind, he only came close to such philosophy when he was flying. Then he felt that his whole body was soaring up into the sky. Man and machine were one. The air, the wind bursting and rushing over the fuselage, brought a new meaning to his life. Such thoughts subsided as quickly as they had arisen when he touched the tarmac—"back to earth," as Smirnov often joked.

Nikolai's reverie was short-lived, for the logic of his mind kicked in with a vengeance. He suddenly felt a terrible burning anguish in the pit of his stomach. His world, that he had known all his life, had gone irrevocably and incomprehensibly mad. Everything was upside down and wrong. *I have to snap out of this nightmare and get back to base as soon as possible.* And yet, for the first time, he had an equally irrational desire to stay and savor the experience of the Mountain as long as possible, not to lose what he had found here with Natasha and the old grandfather. He knew that he would have to return to the reality of the Imperial Air Force. In a peculiar way, his yearning for normality was being seriously challenged. It was beginning to lose its original attraction.

Nikolai walked the length of the meadow and then scrambled onto a tall rock and gazed out across the Mountain. A few feet higher from where he was standing, another strange sight met his eyes. It was a wall of pillow-shaped rocks. It sparkled white in the sunshine. They seemed strangely familiar. He had seen such rock formations before. *But where?* Then he remembered. They had been on the bottom of the Black Sea. He had been snorkeling with comrades from the Corps of Engineers. Atanasov, who had studied geology, identified them as pillow rocks formed from lava quenched by cold seawater. The rocks of this wall on the Mountain were rounded, as if a great sea had shaped them. *It's probably feldspar, white granite,* thought Nikolai. He climbed down from the rock and crossed to the strange wall before him. The surface was crumbling in places, and Nikolai instinctively bent down and rubbed his fingers along the surface of the rocks. He licked his fingers. They tasted of salt. As he continued to examine the surface of the wall, he identified sea shells embedded in the rock. *This is at an altitude of 8,000 feet.* The legend of the ark came to mind. *No, this is nonsense. It is sheer superstition.* Yet he knew that these were pillow rocks, basalts that had either erupted from a vent beneath water or had flowed into water. The lava deposit had been subsequently uplifted by tectonic activity.

Nikolai suddenly realized that he had lost the track. It had ended at the alpine meadow. *Which way now?* He knew he had to head east. To the right of the white rocks, he saw what looked like the beginning of another track that ran up towards the summit of the Mountain. Nikolai scanned the area. This track was the only one visible. Like the one he had already ascended it forced its way through the inhospitable shrub and rock. He decided to follow it. He must have been climbing for at least an hour when he found he had reached the tree line.

It was becoming more difficult as the air grew thinner. Ahead of him, and some two thousand feet higher, Nikolai could make out a cluster of black dots, probably nomad tents, not far short of the snowline. To the east he could make out a track that wound parallel to the twin peaks of Ararat. It was on this track that he expected to catch up with Natasha. She was nowhere to be seen. *She must have climbed with great energy. Even if she were an hour ahead of me, she should be visible by now.* Nikolai cupped his hands over his eyes and searched the track as it wound into the distance. Then he caught sight of a movement. However, it was not on the track, but slightly below. It was a figure too distant to make out whether it was a man or a woman. It was moving with ease across the scattered rock outcrops below the track. Judging from the distance where Nikolai stood, the figure was too tall to be Natasha. Nikolai watched it as it moved deftly across the scree, and then it was gone.

In two hours the sun would be setting. Nikolai had an urge to follow and see if he could find Natasha before he made his way up to the glacier. With this in mind, he doubled his effort and headed east along the track.

# CHAPTER TEN

**A**HMET ALI TOOK Tabrik and four Azeris and headed towards the spot where he had seen the smoke on the ridge. The slopes were mist-covered but did not pose a danger as long as they moved cautiously and kept together. The captain's plan was to reconnoiter what he took to be either a nomad's camp or, even better, a pilot in distress, who had probably lit a fire to keep warm. He hoped for the latter. Stealth was paramount. They did not want to engage the nomads if they could avoid it.

As they approached their target, they came across an alpine meadow. Amidst the green sward, rocks protruded at irregular intervals, like toy blocks abandoned long ago by a giant's child. To the east of the meadow a narrow path cut its way up a steep, rocky embankment. It was bounded by stunted oaks and acacia bushes. The path climbed up the embankment, which in turn rose up out of the trees. Ahmet Ali could see that at the top the ground became rockier and the oaks gave way to stunted alpine spruce.

Ahmet Ali and his men climbed the track until they had reached a spot where it leveled out. It had been almost a vertical climb. Fortunately, protruding rocks and the roots of the alpine spruce provided handholds. The captain stopped to get his breath. He did not want to stop and rest. He silently signaled to his men to continue. It had now turned cold. A sharp breeze blew down from the Mountain, and a mist began to rise up from the Ahora Gorge that lay to the west.

The going was easier once the path leveled out. As they walked slowly along, Ahmet Ali caught the sweet odor of wood smoke. After a few moments, its pale haze appeared above a sod-covered roof that rudely jutted out from the vertical face of an enormous, jagged rock. As they drew nearer, they could see a wooden cabin built into the entrance of a cave. The front of the cabin was covered with lichen and moss, blending subtly into the rock above the cave.

The captain held up his hand and brought the men to a halt. *This is better than I expected. Whoever lives here is no nomad or Kurd. There is only one, tiny door. But just in case, it would be wise to check and see if there is a side entrance. The cabin was built into a cave. It could have escape tunnels, which would allow those who live there to escape. There is nothing I can do about that.*

He ordered the men to fan out. He and Tabrik would storm the cabin. The others were to watch for any escapees. "If anyone tries to escape, shoot them!" The captain held up his hand and then charged forward towards the cabin, revolver cocked at the ready. Reaching the small door, he ducked and kicked it violently. The door was not locked and shot open on impact. The captain, followed by Tabrik, burst in.

Inside the cabin, it was dark, save for the flicker of oil lamps in the far corner of the cabin. The captain swung his revolver around in an arc as he searched for likely inhabitants. The Azeri covered the captain, rifle at the ready. Ahmet Ali stopped dead in his tracks. Sitting calmly on a wooden bench was an old man, who looked up and smiled. The captain had seen that weather-beaten face with its piercing blue eyes before. In a flash, his mind went back to the time when he was a young lieutenant with the Turkish Gendarmerie. *Yes, he has aged, but the expression on the old man's face is unmistakable and familiar. This is the eccentric Russian soldier whom I detained near the border many years ago. The Russian had his grandson with him, a mere boy at the time.* The captain remembered handing his prisoners over to the commandant, who for some unknown reason had allowed them to continue on their journey. Now, here was the same old man, sitting in a cabin on Ararat.

The captain's spoken Russian was limited, but he knew enough to interrogate prisoners. "Who are you?" he demanded. "What are you doing here?"

# CHAPTER TEN

"My name is Simeon, my friend." The old man looked from the captain to Tabrik. "What can I do for you?"

"Do for me?" The captain waved his revolver angrily in the old man's face. "I want to know how you came to be living here!"

"That's simple. I got permission from your commandant." The old man had clearly recognized Ahmet Ali after all those years. His eyes sparkled with mirth as he calmly observed the captain.

"I haven't time to waste, old man. We want that pilot!"

"He's not here."

"So you know whom I mean?"

"Yes."

Ahmet Ali felt his face turning bright red. "Well, where he is?"

"He's gone up the Mountain. What do you want with him?"

"Are you a fool? He's an enemy."

"He's your enemy on the great plain below." Simeon spoke slowly. "Up here, he is our guest."

"What do you mean?" roared the captain. "I can shoot you for this!"

"This is the Holy Mountain of Noah. This is a place of refuge and sanctuary."

Tabrik apparently understood Russian, for he groaned and muttered a prayer in his native dialect.

Ahmet Ali spun around in frustration. "Not you too, you fool." The captain shook with anger.

"Get outside and alert the others. Tell them to take cover. And then return to me. I want that pilot alive when he returns."

Tabrik lowered his rifle and left the cabin to join the others outside. The captain turned to face Simeon. "You are an enemy too, old man. You have been harboring a fugitive." The captain's eyes bulged as he said this. "I can shoot you for this."

"You won't be shooting anyone, my friend."

The captain straightened his tunic and drew himself up to his full height. "I am ordering you in the name of the Sultan to cooperate. This is Ottoman territory. I intend to capture that pilot, and you will help me to detain him."

"I won't help you do anything to harm anybody, my friend."

Ahmet Ali was stunned by the old man's words. Never before had anyone dared to question his orders. This was Turkish territory, and Captain Ahmet Ali was the enforcer of the Sultan's will. "I'll ask you again. Where are you hiding the pilot? If you don't cooperate, I will shoot you and burn down your cabin."

"I have already told you. He's gone up the Mountain."

"Then I'll wait for him to return," the captain said, sitting down on a chair by the table. He placed his revolver on the table and looked searchingly at Simeon. "I don't know what you are doing here, but I am arresting you and that enemy pilot. This time, there is no commandant to turn a blind eye."

Simeon just shrugged.

Ahmet Ali was convinced that he had uncovered a spy hideout. The old Russian, seemingly harmless, was in fact a Russian spy. The fact that the pilot had taken refuge in his cabin was proof enough. The captain would wait for the return of the pilot and then he would arrest both Russians and bring them before the Pasha. The reward would be considerable. Ahmet Ali at last would be rid of the mercenary rabble he was forced to command. He would no longer have to serve out his days in this desolate wilderness. Yes, great things were in store for him. *About time too,* he thought.

Tabrik returned as ordered. His expression was that of fear. He gripped his rifle so tightly that his knuckles showed white against his brown skin.

The captain looked up at the soldier scornfully and then turned to Simeon once more. "I'll ask you again. What are you doing here?" He did not expect a truthful answer, but he believed he might uncover more if he probed long enough. "Where is that grandson of yours?"

The old man ignored the last question. "I live here with God and the people of the Mountain." Simeon closed his eyes for a brief moment. "You should not have come, my friend. This Mountain will be your grave."

"Don't threaten me, you old fool. I don't believe in curses and evil spirits!"

"Because you don't believe in the power of evil, it will overcome you, even if it has not done so already."

# CHAPTER TEN

The captain's face turned purple with rage and the Azeri shifted his feet nervously.

Ahmet Ali suddenly picked up his revolver from the table and pointed it at the old man. "Where is the pilot? This is your last chance," he growled.

"I told you. He has gone up the Mountain."

Shaking with rage, Ahmet Ali went over to Simeon and pressed the muzzle of the revolver against the old man's cheek.

"Don't kill him, Offendi!" Tabrik cried in terror.

The moment that the barrel touched Simeon, an excruciating pain shot up Ahmet Ali's arm. He tried to scream. His face twisted silently, in agony. Beads of sweat ran down his face. He could not utter a sound. The revolver had in that instant become a piece of hot iron in his hand. It seared his flesh. In agony, Ahmet Ali tried to drop it, but he could not release his grip on the handle; his hand remained clenched in a tight grip. His whole body was wracked with pain. The captain gasped for air. Then, in the same moment, it was over.

"Sit down, Captain!" Simeon indicated a spot next to him on the bench.

Involuntarily, Ahmet Ali sat down on the bench next to the old man. He was shaking and sweating profusely. Without thinking, he replaced his revolver back into the holster. He examined his hand. It was red and swollen, but the skin showed no sign of burns. "I can have you shot as a spy," said the captain feebly.

"I don't think your men will oblige,"

Ahmet Ali stared at the old man. He looked at this hand once more. It appeared normal; yet the burning sensation and the pain had been real enough. This was something outside Ahmet Ali's experience. *I must pull myself together.* He stood up, straightened his tunic, and moved to the door of the cabin. He looked back at the old man. He sat in silence. His head was bent on his chest. He appeared as if the incident with the revolver had never occurred. He did not even seem aware of the captain standing there. Silently, Ahmet Ali signaled to Tabrik to follow him.

They went outside, where the other men stood guard. "I want you to stay here and wait for the return of the pilot," the captain said, pointing at three of the Azeris. "When he returns, I want him brought to me. And I want him unharmed!"

"And where will you be, Offendi?" one of the men asked.

"I'll be back with the horses at the first camp." With that, the captain and Tabrik and the other Azeri set off to rejoin the patrol.

# CHAPTER ELEVEN

NIKOLAI HAD NOT gone more than half an hour when he was forced to come a halt. Across the track lay a huge boulder, eight feet in height. *Probably one of those bombs that Simeon mentioned,* he thought. Nikolai could imagine it smashing its way down the Mountain, finally coming to a halt on the track before him. Because of the difficult terrain on either side of the track, he could not go around it, so he was forced to scale it. Finding a hand hold, he hoisted himself up onto the boulder, rested for a moment on top, and then slid down the other side to land on the damp earth of the track once more.

As he straightened up, he froze. Standing a few feet away was the figure of a very tall, dark-skinned man, who was sporting an enormous handlebar moustache. He wore a black sheepskin waistcoat and a maroon felt cap pulled down over his ears. He could have been a monk from a Nestorov painting, save for the rifle that he was pointing at Nikolai. As Nikolai stood rooted to the spot, he felt the tip of a knife pricking the small of his back. Another Kurd had appeared from nowhere and was standing behind him.

"Don't shoot!" Nikolai cried, raising his hands in submission.

The man with the rifle frowned and took aim.

"Don't shoot. I'm a guest of Simeon!"

"Simeon?" The man hesitated for a brief moment and then lowered his rifle.

"Yes, Simeon." Nikolai waved his hand in desperation down the way he had just come.

"You Russkie?"

"Yes!"

The tall Kurd stepped forward. He looked in Nikolai's face and sized him up like a horse at country market. His long, calloused fingers touched Nikolai's blonde hair as if he were examining a horse's mane. He had piercing black eyes, flecked with gray. Nikolai felt his heart turn to water inside him. The Kurd scanned Nikolai from head to toe, as if searching for possible defects. "You come, Russkie!" he ordered, slinging his rifle over his shoulder and turning to lead the way up the track. The other man, behind Nikolai, stepped forward, brandishing a long, curved knife. He grinned at Nikolai and put his knife back into its sheath, which he wore on a belt slung low from his breeches. He was slightly shorter than the other man but taller than Nikolai by at least an inch. He had a mean, pock-marked face and close-set, jet-black eyes. Nikolai was not going to argue.

The taller Kurd led the way, with the other man walking beside Nikolai. They walked in silence, although Nikolai could sense that the Kurd beside him wanted to make conversation. He smiled from time to time, pointing up towards the snow line. To Nikolai, it was apparent that he was being led to the nomad camp higher up the Mountain. *So these are the ferocious Hasasori Nomads, the guardians of the Holy Mountain,* he thought. Luckily for Nikolai, Simeon had been right, although he had not really doubted the old man's reputation among the nomads. To the Kurds, Simeon was a descendent of Noah and Nikolai was his guest.

After another hour's climb, they reached a grassy plateau. Here was a small Hasasori camp. It consisted of black sheep's wool tents scattered around a central tent that was about 40 feet square. Smoke rose from a hole in the main tent, and Nikolai could hear the voices of children laughing and shouting.

It was already late afternoon by the time they arrived at the camp. Behind them, Nikolai could see the brown flat plains below and to the east, a hazy line of hills in the distance that marked the border with Persia. There were no guards posted outside the camp. It was not necessary, for as they approached the camp, four huge grizzly dogs dashed out to meet them, snarling and barking as if they would tear the men to pieces. The pock-faced Kurd quickly bent down and picked up a rock, which he skillfully aimed at the lead dog. It hit the creature on the snout. The dog yelped and turned tail, with the other three following him. Nikolai wondered if one had to run the gauntlet of these fierce canines whenever anyone returned to camp. He looked questioningly at the pock-faced Kurd, who was chuckling to himself.

"Bad dogs. But protect us and sheep from volves and medvedi." As he said this he made a forward slashing movement with his arms like a bear.

"Understood!" Nikolai took in a deep breath.

The Hasasori seemed to be expecting a guest, for as Nikolai was ushered into the main tent he saw that a large bowl of icy cold water had been set out for the weary feet of the arrivals. Nikolai removed his boots and socks and stepped into the bowl. The cold of the Mountain water felt invigorating and refreshing.

A young man, probably Nikolai's age offered him a towel. He said, "My name is Mehmet."

"I'm Nikolai."

"This is Nuri." Mehmet pointed to the pock-marked Kurd. The Kurd smiled, showing a mouth of broken, brown-stained teeth. "And this is my mother, Solmaz." An elderly woman squatted at the fire in the center of the tent making tea. She turned at the sound of her name and nodded.

"And I am Kelim," announced the Kurd with the huge moustache and maroon felt cap. By the respect shown to him, Nikolai guessed that he must be the chief of these nomads. Other men and women sat on soft mats around the fire. They stared fixedly at the Russian visitor, but it was Kelim's eyes that scrutinized him, assessing and weighing up this guest from the outside world. Kelim had eyes that melted Nikolai's nerves. His look was like a fine blade, piercing Nikolai's thoughts. The other men and women were not introduced, but Nikolai nodded politely in their direction. He was then shown to a mat, and a glass of tea was placed before him. Nikolai wanted to ask where Natasha was, but he felt that it was better to wait until the formalities were over.

"We were expecting you." Mehmet smiled at Kelim.

Nikolai did not understand how they had known he was coming. *Natasha could not have told them. Of course,* he thought, *they would have spotted me on the track, but they could not have seen me set out in the early hours of the morning.*

"One of the children," explained Mehmet, "has been staring down the Mountain all morning. She only does this when strangers are climbing the Mountain."

No sooner had Nikolai finished the tea and placed the empty glass down than it was immediately recharged and placed back in front of him. After four refills, Nikolai decided to leave the last glass untouched. Then he noticed that the others lay their glasses down sideways to signal that they did not want any more. He emptied his glass and did likewise. This was a signal for the next course.

Solmaz got up and poured a creamy liquid into a bowl. She beckoned Mehmet, who took the bowl and placed it before Nikolai. The bowl was filled with *yurt,* a watery yogurt drink made from sheep's milk. There was a strong cheese flavor to it that stuck to his palette. He decided to drink it quickly so as not to prolong the experience. When he finished, Solmaz immediately called for the bowl and refilled it, this time right to the brim. Mehmet had great difficulty carrying it to Nikolai without spilling it. Nikolai sipped at the yurt slowly this time.

*Still no sign of Natasha,* Nikolai thought. He looked around at the faces of the Hasasori, all regarding him with fascination. Solmaz appeared to be the oldest member of the family. Her face was etched with deep lines and creases. Her eyes had a grayish look about them, suggesting cataracts. Two young boys of about seven years old had come and squatted very close to him and regarded him inquisitively. When Nikolai stared back at them, they looked to their mothers for reassurance and then smiled at him. One of the boys had hair that was a mousy color that peeped out from under a cap of sheep's wool. His eyes were almond-shaped, giving him an almost Mongolian appearance. The other boy had darker hair, darker skin, and wore a similar cap. He was not so quick to smile as his companion. Their clothes were bright, but a little on the grubby side. However, their faces and hands were spotlessly clean. The two together conjured in Nikolai's mind, an image of wild children of the Mountain.

The communal tent in which they were sitting was made from goat and sheep skins, suspended on supports over a dry stone enclosure. The stonewalling looked very precarious, as if the slightest touch would precipitate a chain of events that could easily result in broken bones. Nikolai was careful not to sit near it.

A younger woman squatted in the corner by a large bowl full of dough and busied herself making flatbread. She carefully and skillfully rolled and flipped the dough into wafer-thin forms and cast it on a red-hot steel dome that rested over a small fire. The fire was fed with dried sheep dung, and the woman periodically fanned the flames with the edge of her skirt. It seemed to Nikolai like hot, uncomfortable, painstaking work, and at times, she looked like she'd rather be anywhere other than there. Occasionally, smoke filled the tent, but no one complained. By the time the dough had all been used, there were over a hundred flatbreads piled on the floor.

As if reading Nikolai's mind, Mehmet pointed at the bread, "This food for family for three days."

"Three days?"

"Yes. But not just the bread. Also mutton and yurt." Mehmet picked up a hot flatbread and offered to Nikolai. It was too hot to eat, and Nikolai placed it on the mat beside him. He hoped this was not disrespectful. Nobody seemed to notice, and in the mean time, Mehmet had gotten up and gone to the entrance of the tent. "Ah ha," he cried.

Nikolai looked up to see Natasha standing at the entrance of the communal tent. She was wrapped from head to heel in a long, black shawl. Nothing showed but her green eyes. But it was Natasha. Nikolai's heart quickened.

She smiled and came over to where he sat. Sitting down next to him, she took his hand and gazed into his eyes, letting the shawl fall around her shoulders.

Nikolai's heart melted. Her touch filled his whole body with warmth. *If only you could speak,* he thought. *Surely something can be done to bring back your speech?*

The formalities being over, most of the Hasasori had gotten up and left the communal tent. Nikolai and Natasha were left alone, save for the woman who had made the bread. Rising from the mat, Nikolai instinctively offered Natasha his arm and pulled her to her feet. She wrapped the shawl around her body but did not cover her head this time. Nikolai led her out of the tent. It was far too late to continue his climb up to the glacier. He imagined that as a guest it was up to him whether he stayed or not. He would have to spend the night here. But for the moment, he desperately wanted to walk alone with Natasha. Speech or no speech, he wanted to share the beauty of the Mountain with her.

At the entrance to the tent, they came across Mehmet, who was filling some Hessian sacks with wool. "Do not go too far from camp. Dogs don't recognize smell and attack you."

Nikolai did not relish the thought of being torn to shreds by these animals. Natasha did not seem concerned, but then the dogs most likely knew her. She was part of the Mountain. Bearing the caution of Mehmet in mind, Nikolai walked with Natasha across the plateau to watch the setting sun. Ararat rose majestically, bathed in the late sunshine. The safest thing was to stay in sight of the camp and the dogs that appeared to be sleeping in a group near one of the smaller tents.

They walked across the plateau towards a cliff that marked its edge. The cliff dropped several hundred feet to a rushing torrent, fed by the melting snow above the plateau. Nikolai and Natasha walked side by side. Nikolai was stunned by her beauty. It was not just her green eyes, which in the light of the late afternoon sun reflected the color of the meadow underfoot; nor was it her sweet, slightly turned-up mouth and the shock of black hair that hung freely about her shoulders. It was the light in her expression, which seemed to glow from deep within her. She was no ordinary person. Nikolai was seeing her for the first time.

Turning to her, he took her hand. She did not resist. The contact filled Nikolai with an inner warmth and joy once more. "Natasha. Do you understand what I say?

Natasha nodded in agreement.

"I wish you would speak to me."

Natasha's expression clouded for a second. She turned away and looked into the distance, but she did not withdraw her hand.

Nikolai knew he had trodden on sacred ground. Nevertheless, he felt he must continue the journey into Natasha's private world. He was convinced that she had the ability to speak. He could not ignore that.

This was another thing that did not make sense in this topsy-turvy world on the Mountain.

To their left, the plateau sloped gently down to a track that wove down to the base of the cliff. Just a few yards to the right of this track, a stream hurried among the rocks in its quest to join the rushing torrent below. Nikolai noted that there were many small brooklets that converged on the waters below the cliff. He and Natasha headed in that direction. They stopped as they reached a spot where the plateau sloped to the track below. Natasha withdrew her hand from Nikolai's and cupped her hands to protect her eyes from the bright light of the sun. She began to search for something in the contours of the Mountain, where they swept down to meet the foothills below. She seemed so absorbed, as if she had forgotten that Nikolai was standing there next to her. Then she dropped hands, sighed, and took his hand again.

One moment Nikolai was beside her, then the next he had spun her around into his arms. Pulling her close to his chest, he kissed her on the lips. Natasha became like wax in his embrace. He had never kissed a girl on the lips before. He had stolen a kiss on the cheek from the young ladies at the annual St. Tatiana's Ball in St. Petersburg, but he had never kissed anyone like he kissed Natasha. Natasha kept her eyes closed but did not push away from him.

They were rudely thrust apart by the snarl and barking of one of the camp dogs. It was bearing down on them at breakneck speed. Nikolai turned in alarm to face the beast. The dog did not stop, but ran straight past them. Nikolai hugged Natasha. She was shivering. Then he saw the target of the savage brute. It was a brown bear, a juvenile that was now loping on all fours hurriedly down the slope in front of them. The dog suddenly came to a halt, turned, and bounded towards them. Natasha pulled herself away from Nikolai. The dog dashed up to her and crouched at her feet. She stooped down and ran her fingers through its thick fur. The dog blissfully thumped its tail heavily on the turf. Nikolai kept still and watched in amazement. The dog then stood up, emitted a rumbling sound deep in its throat, and ran back to the camp.

"You certainly have a way with dogs." Nikolai took a deep breath.

Natasha smiled at him and then came and took his arm. They walked a little way down the slope.

Nikolai suddenly stopped and, sitting on the turf, pulled Natasha gently down beside him. "Let's sit here for a while before we have to return to the camp. The dogs obviously approve of our friendship."

Natasha closed her eyes for a brief moment and then, hugging her knees, sat and surveyed the view with Nikolai.

"I know you can speak," he said wistfully.

Natasha snuggled closer and rested her head on his cheek.

The afternoon passed quickly, and as the sun began to drop behind the Mountain, Nikolai and Natasha returned to the camp. It was time for supper. Solmaz had prepared a mutton stew with rice, bread, and a generous measure of yurt. Kelim, as headman, offered up a prayer and then held out his hands while a young boy poured water over them from a brass pitcher. He shook them dry and then sat down to eat. The bowl was then offered to Nikolai.

"This water from snow on the Mountain. We wash our hands, faces, and chest with the snow. It comes from holy place," explained Mehmet, who had taken on the task of interpreter.

After each man had washed his hands, the women followed, led by Natasha. The whole company ate in silence, although most eyes were on Nikolai and Natasha. Nikolai ate with relish. The mutton stew was very delicious. Even the yurt complimented the meat, even though he was not happy with the large dollops that had been added to his bowl. Solmaz watched to make sure their guests were well provided for and happy with the hospitality.

Nikolai turned to Mehmet, who was sitting a few feet away. "Thank you for your hospitality. The food is excellent. This is the best meal I have had in years."

Mehmet, who spoke a few words of Russian, translated Nikolai's word for Kelim. It was not accurate, but the sentiment was there.

Kelim, whose expression had been grim since he had escorted Nikolai to the camp, now lit up. He grinned, displaying an assortment of wooden and stained broken teeth. Scooping out the last of the yurt and placing the empty bowl on the mat next to him, Kelim addressed Mehmet in Kurmanji.

Mehmet turned to Nikolai. "Chief says, 'It is great honor that you eat with us.'" Kelim smiled and added something further in Kurmanji.

"Not very often we have a Russkie visitor." Mehmet looked at Natasha. "We have our beloved daughter Natasha always," translated Mehmet.

Nikolai bowed graciously to his host and then ate his meal slowly. He did not want to give the impression that he had not been given enough.

When everyone had finished eating, the young women of the company collected the bowls and went away to wash them while Solmaz served tea. After drinking four glasses, Nikolai laid his glass on its side. Natasha kept hers, and for some reason unknown to Nikolai, her glass was not replenished.

Having sat and talked for a while, all the nomads, save Mehmet, quietly left the tent. It was then that Nikolai noticed for the first time that Mehmet was wearing a small, dark brown stone. It was encased in silver, attached to a silver chain around his neck. He knew that many Muslim men wore talismans to protect themselves from evil influences. Seeing that Mehmet was friendly, Nikolai decided to ask him about the stone. "What kind of stone is that, Mehmet?"

"Stone?"

Nikolai pointed to the talisman around Mehmet's neck.

"Oh, this ..."

Mehmet pointed up in the direction of the glacier.

"You found it up there?" Nikolai looked in the direction that Mehmet was pointing.

"No. Not found." Mehmet's Russian was inadequate to make any sense, and after gesticulating with his hands, he removed the talisman and handed it to Nikolai.

As Nikolai examined it, he noticed that the surface of the dark brown stone was warm like amber to the touch. Nikolai realized that it was not a stone after all but some other durable material. "Where did you find it?"

Mehmet made a hollow shape with his hands.

*Does he mean a cave?* thought Nikolai. "A cave?"

Mehmet shrugged. Then he pointed at the fire that was still burning in the middle of the tent.

*No,* thought Nikolai, *he's not going to be able to tell me with his limited Russian.* He turned the talisman over. *The silver is very old, probably antique.* There were marks like some kind of stick writing on the back. They reminded him of primitive cave writing he had once seen in a cave in the Caucasus. He fingered the black substance. *What does this remind me of?* He knew he had seen something similar before, but he could not recall what. Nikolai's reflections were suddenly interrupted by the noisy arrival of a young Hasasori carrying a goatskin gaval. He grinned at Mehmet and shouted something unintelligible to Nikolai.

Mehmet stood up. "Nikolai! Come and join us!" Mehmet looked at Natasha, who, bright-eyed, nodded in agreement.

Together they arose from their mats and went outside into the evening air. A gabus moon had risen, bathing the landscape in an eerie light. There was serenity in the camp. Against the backdrop of darkness, the Hasasori sat, gathered in a circle. The young nomad began to beat out a steady rhythm. The women formed an inner circle and began to follow each other in a line dance. The beauty of the graceful movement of the dancers enthralled Nikolai. He gently squeezed Natasha's hand. The rhythm of the gaval against the silence of the Mountain, the latter now shrouded in darkness, spoke to something deep within him. It was the heartbeat of the earth. It echoed the rhythm of living things, of the trees, the animals, the pastures, and these primitive people who inhabited this precious piece of earth. *Yes, this is precious,* thought Nikolai. He turned and looked at Natasha. Her eyes were fixed on the circle of dancers. Sensing his look, she turned and gazed into his eyes. Then she released her hand and stood up. As she did so, the women, as one body, suddenly opened their ranks. Natasha skipped lightly over the grass and took her place in the circle. The dance resumed, and Natasha was caught up in the movement of the graceful dancers.

The rhythmic beat of the drum stopped, and the women broke the circle and went and sat in a group to one side. The men now formed a new circle, with Kelim in the middle. They began to clap their hands in imitation of the gaval, and Kelim began to dance. His steps were graceful, but unlike the women, his movements were strong and masculine. This was a warrior's dance. The other men did not join in the dance but provided a curious rhythm with their hands. The young boy with the gaval sat silently, watching with the children, who had formed their own group. Mehmet, who was clapping with the other men, suddenly turned and beckoned Nikolai to join them. Feeling somewhat embarrassed, Nikolai nevertheless obliged and went and joined the circle. He sincerely hoped that he would not be required to join in a dance. Although he was a proficient dancer at the annual balls, he did not see himself acting out the role of a Hasasori warrior. Much to his relief, he was only invited to join in the rhythmic clapping, which he managed quite well, although the rhythm was unfamiliar.

After dancing for what seemed like hours to Nikolai, the group dispersed to the main tent. Then the men began to sing. The women did not stay but went immediately to their own tents, leaving Natasha with Nikolai. By the light of the fire, some youths sat around a boy who was carving a large piece of smooth wood, which was longer than his arm. Since there were no trees at this altitude, Nikolai wondered how he had come by such a large piece. Strolling over to see what the boy was carving, Nikolai was startled to see that it was a piece of the propeller from his SB-6. On seeing Nikolai, the boy said something in Kurmanji, pointing over his shoulder.

"Seljan found it up on the glacier, Kolya." Mehmet had appeared, unnoticed by Nikolai. "It's from the great object that fell out of the sky. We are going to carve a Pokrov—a protection."

"Protection?"

"To keep us safe."

Nikolai assumed Mehmet was referring to a talisman, some magical shape that warded off the evil eye. He knew that it was forbidden by their faith to carve images. If they had been literate, someone would have carved a verse from the Koran. What they were going to carve instead, Nikolai had no idea.

"And to thank Allah and the Mountain," added Mehmet. Nikolai looked puzzled, so Mehmet continued.

"The Mountain protects us, and we protect this holy place from intruders. We will add our protection to those already here on the Mountain."

"There are others?" Nikolai looked at the faces around the fire.

"Yes, especially in the ground." Mehmet hollowed his hands as he said this. "There are some on the rocks too. Very old. Perhaps in the time of Nuh."

Nikolai pointed to Mehmet's talisman around his neck. "Like yours?"

"Yes," Mehmet smiled. His fingers automatically touched the strange, dark brown stone in its silver encasement. He held it up to the light of the fire.

Nikolai wanted to explain that the great object from the sky was in fact his plane. But he hesitated. The nomads would not understand his Russian, but more importantly, they might not like the fact that he had been flying in it! *Best to leave this alone. If they believe it was a blessing, then so be it.* He now felt even more determined to climb up to the glacier. He would take Natasha with him. He just needed to get a good night's sleep.

A cold wind began to blow across the plateau. Gusts began to tug at the ropes of the tent. The men stopped singing and as one body rose and went off to their respective beds. Natasha stood up and went to join the other women. The boys too got up and went off to their tents. Nikolai found himself sitting alone in the communal tent.

"It's time to sleep," Mehmet said, entering the tent, his arms full of sheepskins. Nikolai had not noticed him slip out of the tent. He had been engrossed with watching the boy carving.

"I would like to take a stroll in the moonlight before I sleep."

Mehmet's face immediately dropped at this simple request. His cheerful expression was replaced by a look of uneasiness. He paused for a moment, and then said, "But don't go too far or stay out too long." Then he added, as an afterthought, "The dogs might become restless and attack you."

Nikolai did not need to be reminded. He had noticed the dogs watching him earlier. It seemed to him that they were only waiting for an opportunity to catch him on his own. Natasha had already gone to bed; otherwise he would have invited her to walk with him. He so much wanted to step out into the moonlight, especially up here at this altitude. The view would be breathtaking. *It will only take a few minutes,* he thought. *I'll walk just to the edge of the camp and then come straight back.* "I won't go far, Mehmet."

"Please do not stay for too long." There was urgency in his voice.

Nikolai found it odd that Mehmet was worried about his staying out in the night air. *Is it because of the cold? It is cold, for sure. No. Mehmet's expression spoke of something that could not be spoken.* "I'll be quick," Nikolai promised. He pulled down his cap over his ears and stepped into the cold night air. He walked across the soft grass of the plateau, almost to the spot where he had seen the young bear. But he stopped a few yards before the spot and gazed up at the Mountain bathed in the moonlight. The snow on the twin peaks sparkled like a myriad of tiny stars. The lower slopes cast long, eerie shadows. The glacier glowed, reflecting the moonlight like a mirror. Just to his left he noticed an object sitting on a rock. As he approached, he saw that it was a large bowl filled with yurt. *What on earth is this doing here? Are the nomads feeding wild animals?* He did not think so. But there it was all the same, sitting on the rock. It was probably one of their protection rituals. *It will probably be consumed by that young bear we saw earlier,* he thought. Puzzled by the bowl of yurt and the uneasiness of Mehmet, Nikolai headed back to the camp.

Back in the communal tent, Nikolai went and sat down by the fire. It was now simply embers but gave off a pleasant heat all the same. He had barely warmed himself when Mehmet entered the tent and beckoned Nikolai to follow him. Nikolai was ushered to a tent only a few feet away. Inside, there were just two other nomads, who appeared to be fast asleep already. Mehmet offered Nikolai a thick mat to lie on and a large bundle of sheepskins. "You sleep here." Mehmet bowed and left the tent without another word.

Nikolai thought it strange that no one took leave of each other but simply went to bed without saying anything. *But maybe that is their custom,* he thought as he covered himself with the sheepskins. It was cold in the tent, but surely after the day's exhaustion and the fresh air of the Mountain he would sleep soundly. But Nikolai was in for an unpleasant surprise. After half an hour of fitful dozing, he was awakened by more men entering the tent and placing their bedding next to him. They did not speak, but nevertheless, their movements prevented him from getting back to sleep. Finally, he drifted off, only to be awakened by the heavy breathing of the other sleepers. From a sheep pen, he could also hear the persistent coughing of a bronchial ewe. At first he thought it was a person, but then he realized that the coughing was coming from outside the tent. *It does sound strangely human,* he thought. Just before dawn, he finally fell into a deep sleep and, surprisingly enough, awoke later, feeling none the worst for a disturbed night.

Nikolai sat up and stretched. The other occupants of the tent had already gone off presumably to their tasks. Nikolai carefully folded his mat and placed the bundle of sheepskins on top. Then he went outside into the fresh morning air. The green of the plateau had changed to a blinding white. Its brightness made him scrunch up his eyes. There had been a light fall of snow overnight. He was surprised, as there had been no hint in the clear moonlit sky when he had climbed sleepily into his tent. He glanced up at the glacier. It was enveloped in a thick fog. He could hear distant thunder, but he could not see any flashes of lightning. He realized that he and Natasha would not be able to make the ascent after all. *Not this time,* he thought. The snow crunched under his feet as he made his way to the communal tent. Solmaz was already preparing breakfast. She squatted by the fire, stirring a pot.

Nikolai sat down and waited. Within minutes, Natasha appeared. She greeted Nikolai with a smile and then went and filled two glasses of tea. She brought them to the mat and offered a glass to Nikolai. As she offered it to him, Nikolai held his hand over hers for a moment, then gently bent forward and kissed her cheek. Natasha kissed Nikolai on the lips and then quickly glanced in the direction of Solmaz. He could tell she was wondering if Solmaz had seen this intimate exchange. Solmaz continued to stir the pot on the fire, but Nikolai caught a glimpse of her smiling to herself.

Natasha got up and went to help Solmaz. She held out two bowls, which Solmaz filled with porridge. This was topped off with yurt. Natasha returned to Nikolai, and together they ate their breakfast of yurt porridge and bread, followed by several glasses of tea. Solmaz did not join them. She would probably eat later, when the men came to the tent.

Having eaten, they exchanged farewells with their hostess and prepared to set out for the journey back to the cabin. Kelim was nowhere to be seen. Mehmet was, however, standing outside, waiting to accompany them to the edge of the camp. "May Allah go with you!"

Mehmet bowed and made a salaam, touching his forehead and making a sweeping gesture with his hand. "May he give you the strength of a thousand mules."

"It's all downhill from here." Nikolai turned to Natasha and laughed.

Fortunately, the snow was very light, and they barely left footprints in its powdery covering. Nikolai glanced at the large bowl he had seen the night before. It was empty. Something had eaten the yurt in the night. And someone without shoes had left large footprints, which led to the edge of the yavala.

By the time they reached the track that led down to the bottom of the cliff, there was no trace of snow. The earth was wet but not slippery. The morning was still. The Mountain hung in silence. Ararat had not yet arisen from sleep. The sky was cloudy. There was no bird song. The only sound was the distant roar of the torrent of icy water below. Despite the grayness of the morning, Nikolai felt that he had never been so happy in all his life. Even the dull colors of the landscape, which previously would have dampened his spirits, promised a day of joy and happiness. The Mountain, to Nikolai's mind, appeared fresh and welcoming. Soon the sun would break through, bathing the Mountain in a golden light. *This is going to be a day to remember,* he thought.

After an hour, they finally reached the rushing torrent below. The roar of the waters was deafening as they merged from different directions and cascaded into the Mountain river. Nikolai felt thirsty. He beckoned to Natasha and scrambled down the moss-covered rocks to the water's edge. There, he bent down and scooped up the cold, crystal water in his hands. He looked up at Natasha, who was scrambling down too. She came and knelt down beside him, taking a draught of the icy water in her hands. As she drank, Nikolai leaned over and stroked her hair out of her face. Having refreshed themselves, they scrambled back up the rocks to the track.

They continued for another half hour in good spirits. Nikolai was looking forward to a hot meal at the cabin and the comfort of bed. As they journeyed, Nikolai looked up at the sky overhead. Despite his optimism, the sun did not break through. The promise of brightness did not come to fruition. In fact, the sky above them darkened. There was a storm brewing. By now, Nikolai knew that the weather could change in half an hour. Natasha wrapped her shawl around her, this time, covering her head as well. He was glad for the felt cap that Simeon had given him. He pulled it over his ears.

Then it came—a hailstorm—bitter, blinding, and wet. The thorns on the scrub bushes quivered, riddled with icy balls. It was accompanied by a razor-like wind coming off the snow-powdered ridges. They were forced to find shelter quickly. They dashed and crawled under the nearest overhang of rock, where they squatted, waiting for the full force of the storm to abate. Nikolai thought that it would just be a quick hailstorm. It would soon pass. However, this turned out to be wishful thinking on his part, for as if to test his strength further, the hail continued, full force, unabated. The Mountain did not measure out half measures, for the hail was followed by a dragging, gray column of heavy rain that splashed and sprayed up from the track, creating mud holes in the sodden earth. Its impact made the rocks glisten like hammered lead.

The rain, however, only lasted a few minutes, and then it was still. Nevertheless, the sun did not break through. Instead, a heavy fog descended, totally obliterating the track a few yards away. Nikolai and Natasha huddled together for warmth. They were stuck there, wet and shivering. The damp air seemed to penetrate Nikolai's body.

After a few minutes, he had to relieve himself. He felt embarrassed in the company of Natasha. But when nature calls, you have to obey. To make light of it and cover his embarrassment, Nikolai stood up and stretched. "Excuse me, Natasha, for a moment. I have to go where the Tsar does not go on horseback, as they say at the Imperial Court." He did not look at Natasha as he said it, but quickly disappeared into the fog. A little further down the track, he reached a fork in the trail. *Got to remember where I am,* he thought. *I need a marker.* It was then that he saw a white stone to the left of the track. *This will be ideal.* He turned off the track at this point. He would check for the white stone when he returned to Natasha. The fog was so thick by now that he could hardly see past his own hands.

Having satisfied nature, Nikolai returned to the track to find that the white stone was nowhere to be seen. He spun around, searching in the dimness of the fog. *No white stone. I must have passed it when I returned to what I thought was the original track.* He climbed back up the track in the direction that he thought he had come and called out for Natasha. His voice sounded thin in the thickness of the fog. He kept calling and then stopped. *How can Natasha answer? I am a fool. Calling her could cause her leave the overhang and seek my voice. Then we would both be lost.* "Never leave the track," Simeon had warned. Nikolai, in his haste, had ignored this basic rule of the Mountain. Now he was not just hopelessly lost, but he had lost Natasha too. What had begun as a day full of promise was now turning into a nightmare of frustration and danger.

Nikolai was convinced at first that he was returning to Natasha by going back up the track. Although he could not find the white stone, he felt sure he was heading in the right direction and that he would find the overhang of rock where they had taken shelter from the hail and rain at any moment. He walked and called, "Natasha. I'm coming." But the further he walked, the more he realized that he had gone up the wrong track. The fog was too thick for him to retrace his steps. The ground beneath his feet was somehow different. It was rockier. He found himself slipping and sliding on the wet surfaces of rocks that protruded from the track. "Natasha!"

Natasha did, in fact, hear him in the distance. It did not make sense to her since Nikolai had only been gone a few minutes. She crawled out from under the shelter and listened intently.

"Natasha!"

The voice sounded distant. She immediately headed in its direction, forgetting that she should never attempt to move in the fog. But she could not resist Nikolai's call. Soon, however, his words were swallowed up by the fog, and he eventually ceased calling. They had become separated. Fate was cruel. The Mountain was cruel. This precious moment in their lives had been taken from them by the vicissitudes of nature.

Natasha, realizing that she had lost Nikolai, decided to try and head back up the Mountain. The track was steep and slippery, but it wound its way upward. By following it, she hoped to climb clear of the fog bank. From her experience, these fog banks dropped from the higher slopes and settled at a lower altitude. If she could stick to the track and follow its ascent, she thought she would eventually climb out of the fog. Visibility was about fifty feet.

She climbed for at least an hour. It seemed that the fog was preceding her, just keeping slightly ahead. *At least I am on the same track. Thankfully there have been no other intersecting paths that might lead to nowhere.* Of course, she was not sure that this track would be any different, but somehow she felt that she should continue whatever happened. After awhile, the track climbed steeply up between two gigantic boulders, their smooth surfaces painted with yellow lichen. She stopped to get her breath and survey the scene. The bleakness of the scene had its own beauty. The lichen shone like gold against a background of grays and black-brown, with the fog adding mysterious shading. She had become separated from Nikolai. She was concerned but not fearful. It would work out in the end. Saint Nikolai would protect them both.

As if reading Natasha's thoughts, Nikolai too decided to climb up the track, hoping to break free of the fog. He felt desperate. He had lost Natasha, and now he was lost too, due to his lack of thought. He was forced to grope his way without knowing where he was going. Nikolai also had a feeling that he was not alone. The dim outline of rocks suggested strange, nightmarish creatures. But he knew that it was not just his imagination. He had a strong sense that he was being pursued by something that kept its distance whenever he paused to listen. He looked back. There was nothing to be seen in the thick fog.

# CHAPTER TWELVE

"**T**HIS MOUNTAIN WILL be your grave." The words of the old man echoed in Ahmet Ali's brain. No matter how much he tried to suppress them, they kept coming back. He stretched out the fingers on his right hand. They felt normal. There was no muscular damage. *But the pain had been real enough. No, I did not imagine that. Tabrik was a witness. What will the Azeri tell the others when we get back to the patrol?* Ahmet Ali felt cornered. He must not lose control. He had suffered a setback, but he still had a mission to accomplish. He did not believe in the supernatural. There must have been a logical explanation for the strange incident. Ahmet Ali had faced danger in battle. He feared no one. He had always believed that he was master of his own fate. And yet, he knew now that this was not true. He tried to concentrate on the task ahead, on what he would do when he found the wreckage of the enemy plane. But the words of the old man buzzed in his mind like a plague of horse flies.

The group walked in silence. The captain was weary but was careful not to show it. He was a rider, not a foot soldier, and the continuous climbing was beginning to tell on him. After an hour's steady trek, the weather changed abruptly. An icy wind began to blow in their faces. They had to cover their eyes from its bitter blast. It seemed to carry the old man's words with it, for Ahmet Ali began to take stock of the situation once more. *Here was this old Russian fool, boldly living on Turkish territory and openly offering hospitality to an enemy. I could have either waited for the return of the pilot or rejoined my men to search for the wreckage. If the old man was lying, I would have waited at the cabin in vain.* The captain was a man of action. He could not have simply sat and waited. *I made the right decision.* As if to confirm his thoughts, the wind blew harder. Soon his only thought was to take shelter, and having rested, then head back to the patrol as fast as they could.

Along the track, they came across smaller paths that led to a warren of tunnels on either side. Some were suitable for small rodents, others were big enough to house a bear. The captain chose a large cave and decided to take refuge in its entrance. As they entered the cave, a small owl suddenly sped past them like a bullet, causing the Azeris to cry out in alarm. The captain was startled too, not by the fleeing owl, but by this unexpected response from the men. *Are they afraid of a bird?* He suddenly remembered how Javad had jumped back in fear when a similar incident occurred earlier. *Some superstitious nonsense,* he thought bitterly.

They were now in the full force of the storm. Visibility was down to a few feet. Great sheets of freezing hail smashed their way across the entrance of the cave. Bullet-like, they bounced off the sodden earth and ricocheted past the men, landing at some distance behind them. The storm showed no sign of abating. Ahmet Ali and the two Azeris were forced to sit and wait it out. The captain was glad of the rest, but he nevertheless felt an urgency to meet up with the patrol at the first opportunity.

They must have sheltered there for at least half an hour before the hail finally ceased. Then the wind dropped, and a freezing fog settled like a thick, white blanket across the entrance of the cave. Visibility was now down to a foot, if that. The men peered out at the white darkness that hung before them. They would be forced to stay where they were until the fog lifted. The captain felt the hairs on the back of his neck tingle. There was an expectancy that chilled his bones. He removed his Smith and Wesson from its holder and aimed at the entrance. What he expected, he did not know. Tabrik and the other Azeri followed suit, pointing their Mausers as if to repel an invisible enemy. Sweat poured down Tabrik's face. Although nothing was said, they acted as one body, coordinated by fear as they stared fixedly at the whiteness before them.

Like the previous time, when two of the patrol had disappeared, this was no ordinary fog. It was the same chilling breath as before. Ahmet Ali felt its presence enter the cave. The men moaned in terror as it approached, and then as quickly as it had manifested itself, the presence disappeared, although the fog outside the cave remained.

The captain sighed with relief. Tabrik rested his rifle. However, the other Azeri still stood rigid, staring at something only he could see. He muttered something under his breath and then leaned his rifle against the wall of the cave. Still staring at something in the fog, he walked slowly towards the entrance of the cave.

"Firuz!" called Tabrik, lunging forward to restrain him.

The other man pushed Tabrik aside and walked slowly into the fog. Ahmet Ali could just make out his outline for a few seconds before it was swallowed up in the whiteness.

It was several minutes before the captain could find words. "Where has he gone, Tabrik?"

The Azeri did not answer. There was a scowl on this face as he turned to face the captain.

"Well, he's probably gone to relieve himself," suggested Ahmet Ali. "I hope Firuz keeps the cave in sight." The captain's voice sounded weak and unconvincing. "As soon as Firuz gets back, and assuming the fog lifts, we'll be on our way again."

Tabrik nodded and then squatted down beside his rifle.

After a short while, the fog began to lift. The track leading to the cave became visible once more. However, there was no sign of Firuz. The captain stepped outside and called the Azeri. There was no answer. He called several times. Still no answer. Firuz had gone. *Perhaps he has deserted*, he thought. Given the thick fog, it was an ideal opportunity to take off and head back down the Mountain. On the other hand, Firuz must have known how dangerous it would be in zero visibility. Anyway, he had gone. There were now just the two of them. The captain turned to Tabrik, "The fog is lifting, let's go!"

Tabrik picked up his rifle and followed the captain. They resumed their journey, following the main track eastwards. Ahmet Ali wanted to tell Tabrik that it was not his fault that Firuz had walked out on them. It was not his fault that he had already lost two other men and that he'd had to threaten the old man. It was this accursed mountain with its volatile climate and unexpected hazards. He had to do what he had to do. But the captain could not find the words. Besides, the Azeri would not understand. *Best to say nothing.*

The track began to climb steeply. The captain slowed his pace. He was exhausted. He could see that another storm was building up on the slope above them. They were heading it its direction. The captain's heart dropped. There was no shelter to be seen. They would be caught in its onslaught. He did not want to turn back, but there was no choice. He looked at Tabrik and said, "We are not going to make it if we get caught up in that." Ahmet Ali pointed to the heavy clouds that were already rolling down to engulf them. He felt fear welling up inside him. "There's an overhang back down the track. I think we can make it before the storm hits us."

Tabrik did not answer but continued to scowl at the captain. There was a frightening hatred behind it. The captain turned away from the Azeri and took a quick glance at the advancing clouds. They were not going to make it before it hit them. The captain covered his head with his cloak and squatted as low to the ground as he could. "Take cover!"

In that same second, Tabrik raised his Mauser and took aim at the captain. There was a sudden flash and a deafening explosion as a bolt of lightning struck the track. It found the tip of Tabrik's rifle, melted it in an instant, and simultaneously pierced the Azeri through the chest. It continued to sear its way down to the soles of his feet. He dropped onto the icy ground like a felled tree, an unrecognizable heap of charred flesh and bone.

Ahmet Ali remained crouched on the ground as the full brunt of the storm raged around him. This was a battle he was not prepared for. This was a battle with nature, unlike any he had experienced in his years as a soldier. All he could do was remain crouched against the wet earth of the track, with only his cloak for protection. If the lightning struck again, they could be killed too. There was nothing he could do but wait out the fury around him.

Then as quickly as it had vented its wrath, the storm moved elsewhere. There was a silent moment. The immensity of the Mountain shrunk to a single thought in Ahmet Ali's mind. He tried to listen, to work out why fate had done this to him. *Why did it happen like this?* He was blood—a heart beat among the lifeless boulders. *Surely I am of more worth than the Mountain?*

Realizing that the storm had abated, Ahmet Ali abandoned his thoughts, got unsteadily to his feet, and staggered a few steps. A sideway glance revealed the charred remains of the Azeri. The smell of burnt flesh was sickening. Then another sudden explosion set him off, running off the track like a madman—slipping, sliding, and bumping on his back until he was stopped by a large bolder barring his way. He lay there for some time, breathing heavily and vomiting. In the fall he had lost his cap, and his tunic and cloak were now splattered and stained with mud. His hair was disheveled and caked with dirt. He staggered to his feet, feeling for his Smith and Wesson. It was intact in the holster. He pulled it out and wiped it with the silk cloth he kept in the holster. *I must move on. I must take control. I will get back to patrol, whatever happens.* He looked up at the sky above him. The storm had passed. But he knew it could return, or another would brew itself into a front of terror and destruction. "The Mountain will be your grave...." *No! It will not. I shall find the wreckage, and I will return triumphant!*

It was the young Mahmud who first spotted the captain returning to the patrol. At first he could not make out the disheveled figure making its way slowly up to the ridge where they had set up camp. When he realized who it was, he ran to alert the others. Mahmud could not believe his eyes as the captain finally reached the camp. He was soaked to the skin and shivering, his once immaculate tunic and cloak now bespattered with mud. The young Mahmud grabbed a blanket from his pack and, running to meet the captain, wrapped it around him. "I'll fetch some hot tea, Offendi."

Another Azeri led the captain to one of the goatskin shelters and spread out a bed for him to lie on. Ahmet Ali did not resist. He sat there like a drowned marmot, his teeth chattering while he sipped hot tea. No one dared ask him what had happened or where the other men were. They knew that the captain would not have answered if they had asked. He needed to rest and regain his strength. What had happened had happened. He had fared much worse in the heat of battle.

"Good to have you back, Offendi." Mahmud tried to sound cheerful. "Would you like some more tea?"

Ahmet Ali shook his head. After a long silence, he seemed to recover. "Where's Javad?"

"He's further up the track, Offendi," replied Mahmud. "He and Vugor went to reconnoiter the higher slopes."

"Do you have any food?"

"Yes, of course, Offendi." Mahmud smiled at the captain's request. "I'll bring you some broth. We caught some hares, well…three, and they made a good stew." Mahmud was anxious to please the captain. Unlike the other men, he had great admiration for his commanding officer. He hated to see his leader so dejected. "I'll fetch some at once." Mahmud went to fetch some of the stew. He filled a gourd, cut off a chunk of bread, and carefully brought them back to the captain. *This is the last of the stew,* he thought. *Javad and Vugor will have to be content with the dried goat's meat and bread.*

Mahmud thought about how they got the hares. The men had stopped on a ridge to eat their dry rations and clean their rifles. It was while they were occupied that they spotted a group of hares. This was an unusual sight, since hares traveled alone. One of the Azeris was quick in shooting all three, a feat in itself. He had been severely reprimanded by Javad for discharging his Mauser. The volleys had echoed across the slopes. By now their position would have been given away. If there were Kurds in the area, they would soon find out. Still, what had been done had been done.

Javad and Vugor had decided to go further up the track and check the area above them for signs of movement. Javad had ordered the rest of the patrol to rest and await further orders.

"It's in the ravine over there," Javad pointed to a position just left of them.

Vugor nodded and stared hard. However much he screwed up his eyes, he could see nothing, but he knew Javad had seen something. "What do we do now?"

"Nothing, for the moment." Javad seemed deep in thought. He released the safety catch on his Mauser. "Go back and tell the others. I'll stay here and keep watch."

Vugor descended swiftly down the track to where the patrol was resting. He was surprised to see that the captain had returned. And even more surprised to see the mud-stained tunic and disheveled appearance of his superior officer. Ignoring this, Vugor gave his report. "Offendi. Javad has spotted something. I think we are being followed."

"Kurds?"

"No, Offendi. Something else."

"Something else?" The captain glared at Vugor.

"Javad can explain."

Ahmet Ali fingered his revolver and rose to his feet, straightening his tunic. "I need to see this for myself." His voice was grim. At that moment, Mahmud arrived with more hot tea. The captain nodded his appreciation but did not take the glass. "I am going to investigate. I want everyone on full alert."

Mahmud stared at his commanding officer in disbelief. "Forgive me Offendi, but you need to rest." The young Azeri looked at the other men as if for support.

The captain stared back at Mamud but did not answer. He straightened his tunic and rose to his full height. Ignoring Mahmud, he addressed an older Azeri. "Osman! I want you to take command of the patrol while I go and investigate. See to it that the men are ready. I don't want any excuses!"

Turning, the captain accompanied Vugor back up the track. He was still unsteady on his feet and hoped that Vugor had not noticed. But he knew that the Azeri scout missed nothing. However, Ahmet Ali would not give up until he dropped. He summoned his strength and followed the scout, stumbling and slipping on the steep track but managing to keep up all the same.

As they reached the spot where Vugor had left Javad, they saw him crouched beside a cluster of boulders. Javad clambered to his feet. "It's gone, Offendi." Javad pointed at an outcrop of rock to the east of the track.

"What did you see?"

"Nothing. But it's gone."

"I don't understand." The captain scanned the area where Javad had sensed something.

"There was something there, Offendi. I could feel it watching me."

"But it's not there now?"

"No, Offendi."

"Could it have been an animal?" The captain knew that the scout was speaking the truth and that he had sensed something.

"If it was an animal," Javad answered, "why would it be following us? And how has it remained hidden each time."

"It's not a Kurd," Vugor said and spat on the ground.

"Or a Hasasori Nomad," added Javad. "They shoot first. They don't stalk their enemy."

"If it is a spy, you will need to deal with him quietly." The captain looked at Vugor.

Vugor smirked and fingered the pommel of his curved dagger in its sheath.

"Continue to keep watch, all the same. It's getting dark. We will camp here for the night.

"Yes Offendi!"

Vugor looked at Javad questioningly but said nothing. The captain guessed what the scouts were thinking. *This is the forbidden mountain —the sooner we leave the better. We should not be stopping here. But I need to rest. We can continue tomorrow.*

# CHAPTER TWELVE

The captain turned and pointed back down the track. "We had better rest there for night. It's a sheltered place, and we can keep watch from the safety of the rocks."

The captain barely managed to walk back to the camp. He desperately needed rest. It had taken all his strength to climb the track. It was a terrible strain on his body. Having reached the camp, he collapsed once more on the bed provided for him.

That night the patrol made a camp in the shelter of some rocks, close to the track. The ground was damp from the mist. Nevertheless, they managed to make a fire. Two sentries were posted while the rest of the men laid down to sleep, their rifles at the ready.

As Ahmet Ali crawled into his shelter, he felt the hairs on the back of his neck tingle. Something was amiss. He stopped and turned his head slowly. He saw a tall figure hurrying silently down the slope of an adjacent overhang of rock only a few yards from his shelter. Within seconds it had disappeared. Javad had told him that Kurds were too superstitious to attack at night. Whatever or whoever it was, it had gone. He was too exhausted to pursue the matter. However, he took his Smith and Wesson out of its holster, rubbed it with the silk cloth, and placed it next to his head. He then wrapped his fur-lined cloak around his shoulders and buried himself under a pile of sheepskins. Within minutes, he was asleep.

As he slept, he had a dream that he was on parade at the Porte. His tunic was splattered with mud, and he had lost his cap. *Where did I mislay it? I will have to leave the parade ground and find it.* But General Mahmud Mukhtar Pasha was approaching. There was no time to change or find another hat. As he stood in this disheveled manner, the General Pasha came up to him and pinned a medal on his chest.

"Why are you so dirty?" asked the General.

Ahmet Ali tried to explain what had happened but could not find the words.

"Why are you so dirty?" the General asked again.

"I had to catch a spy, Your Excellency!"

"You are exaggerating again," replied the General.

"Yes, he always exaggerates," chorused the men around him on parade. "The Peacock always exaggerates, exaggerates…."

"I don't exaggerate," Ahmet Ali protested. He kept repeating these words until he woke up. He was shivering with cold and reached for another sheepskin in the darkness of the shelter. He managed to find another one and covered himself with it. He lay there thinking of his dream. "I do not exaggerate. They don't understand," he mumbled angrily. After a while, he fell into a restless sleep, tossing and turning. He slept fitfully until dawn.

# CHAPTER
# THIRTEEN

THE PATROL AWOKE to find that a thick fog had descended on the camp during the night. Although it was dawn, visibility was down to a few yards. They would have to wait until the fog lifted. It was then that strange figure appeared again. This time, Ahmet Ali saw it clearly. It was standing only a few yards away, on the track above the camp. At first he thought it was a very tall man, but on closer examination, he could see it was not human, although it had the body of a man. Instead of clothes, it was covered with pelt. Its face was human but much flatter than anyone's he had ever seen before, and it too was covered with a light fluff. The forehead was high and curved, with jutting eyebrows. The nose was small and flat. Its chin was round. But what was most startling was its vacant expression. Its face was that of a creature with no soul. It stood there, its arms hanging by its side. It seemed to be looking straight through Ahmet Ali. The captain instinctively reached for his revolver. As he did so, the creature hissed like a mountain lion. The captain took aim and squeezed the trigger, but nothing happened. The gun had jammed. The creature suddenly dropped onto to all fours and turned and ran swiftly up the track. It was gone as quickly as it appeared, hidden in the fog.

The captain stood there, looking at the spot where the strange creature had been. He had not felt any fear but rather curiosity. What was it? He had heard stories of the Mountain man, a half human creature that was once a man but had had its soul devoured by the evil Shaytan spirit. Of course, all this was nonsense, old women's tales. And yet, here on the track, Ahmet Ali had seen such a humanoid creature, the stuff of legends, with his own eyes.

"Captain!"

The captain's reverie was interrupted by the call of Javad, who was coming down the track. To his amazement, three figures emerged from the fog. Javad was dragging a young woman. Her hands were tied behind her back, and her mouth was gagged.

"Look at what we have found!" Vugor said with a malicious laugh.

"I found her just above our camp." Javad pushed his captive forward.

"She's a spy for sure," added Vugor. "Most likely sent by the Kurds to prepare an ambush."

"I don't think she was the one that was following us. I would have spotted her earlier." Javad wore a puzzled expression. "When I found her, she was not hiding but wandering aimlessly further up the track."

"Probably a decoy," Vugor snarled.

The captain was silent. He could see that this girl was no Kurd. She was Caucasian. He had to weigh up the situation quickly. She was very beautiful, despite her disheveled appearance. She would fetch a good price at the Porte. But to travel with a female captive would not be easy. "What is your name?" Ahmet Ali demanded.

There was no answer. She obviously did not understand Turkish.

"Ask her in your language, Javad."

The scout addressed her in Azeri, but still the girl gave no answer.

Vugor gazed at the girl. "Maybe she doesn't speak," Vugor said mockingly. "I can make her talk, Offendi," he added with a predatory look at the girl.

"I want her in one piece for the moment." The captain was at a loss as to what to do. He had to think hard. *I could get a good price for a female slave. And this girl is obviously of good breeding. Maybe I could get a ransom? But where did she come from?* "Do you speak Russian?" the captain asked in broken Russian.

The girl's eyes registered understanding, but she said nothing.

"Ah, she's a mute—worthless in my opinion," said Vugor. "Better slit her throat here and now and get on with our search."

"A great pity to waste such beauty," Javad said with an evil smile. The other men in the patrol, who had gathered around, laughed.

Despite all his military experience, Ahmet Ali was in a situation in which he did not have an answer. He did not want to kill the girl, but on the other hand, he did not want to be burdened with a female captive. It would cause trouble with the men. The way they had responded to Javad's comment was disturbing. There was the possibility of a reward, but was it worth it? He would have to take her all the way to the Pasha. It was difficult enough to maintain discipline, and with a girl in tow, his job would be much more difficult. Reluctantly, Ahmet Ali agreed that Vugor was right. Better to kill her now and resume the search. The captain paused and then nodded to Vugor. "Do it quickly, but not here."

Nikolai had emerged from the fog to find himself up much higher than he had imagined. He had thought that the track was running parallel to the Mountain, but in fact, it was steadily climbing without his realizing it. There was still no sign of Natasha. In spite of the brilliant sun above, it felt much colder on this part of the Mountain. Nikolai pulled the sheepskin waistcoat tightly around him. A bitter wind began to blow. He pulled his cap further over his ears. The sun suddenly became obliterated by a bank of cloud that rolled swiftly down the Mountain. He decided that he would continue as long as the visibility held. If the worst occurred, he would have to remain where he was until there was a break in the mist. He was not going to repeat that mistake again. *So far, so good,* he thought as he made his way further along the track.

After half an hour, he saw that the mist had completely covered the track ahead. *Well, I'll stop when I can go no further,* he thought. Entering the mist, he stopped and sat to rest on a boulder beside the track. He had to admit that he was lost. If the fog did not lift, he would have to spend the night on the Mountain. *I lost Natasha. She could be anywhere.*

Somehow he knew that she was quite capable of looking after herself. With this comforting thought, he sat and waited for the fog to lift.

He began to think about his squadron. *Did they mount a search for me? Will someone be detailed to fly out to find me? How am I going to explain the crash? No one is going to believe what's happened to me.* He felt frustrated by this, but not fearful as he had been before. Somehow he trusted the old man. Things would work themselves out—maybe not logically as he understood it, but maybe luck or fate or something else beyond his control, would intervene. He had for the first time in his life the feeling that despite the odds stacked up against him, he would pull through. But first he had to find Natasha. He needed her desperately. She was now a part of his life, of his destiny. He stared into the blanket of fog. "How long do I have to wait?" he said out loud.

The answer was a woman's scream, followed by rifle shots.

Vugor dragged Natasha off the track, some yards from the rest of the men. Javad followed at some distance. Finding a spot just above a steep ravine, Vugor threw Natasha to her knees. As she hit the ground, she let out a piercing scream. Vugor quickly pulled out his knife and, seizing her by the hair, bent her head backwards, placing the knife on her naked throat.

As the blade made contact with her skin, a long, drawn-out hiss sounded behind him. Vugor swung around and looked up. Standing over him was a tall figure. Vugor opened his mouth to cry out, but no sound came. In terror, he turned the knife towards the creature, letting Natasha slump to the ground. The creature hissed and struck out at Vugor. A powerful arm knocked the Azeri across the ground, his knife clattering on the rocks as he fell. At the same moment, the creature moved swiftly to the Azeri and hissed, its arms raised to strike once more. Vugor, in an instant, rolled to one side and was on his feet, running blindly into the fog that hung above the ravine. Letting out a blood-curdling cry, he tripped and fell headlong into the abyss below.

The patrol heard Vugor's cry, followed by the crack of rapid rifle shots echoing across the Mountain. There was a moment's silence, followed by a deep rumbling up on the slope above.

"Fall in and follow me!" Ahmet Ali commanded, leaving the track and dashing in the direction of the shots. The patrol followed, each man ready for combat. They were, however, slowed down by a blanket of fog that had settled over the spot where Javad and Vugor had taken the girl for execution. Taking extra caution, the men kept close ranks, staring ahead, ready to shoot. Just as they were about to fire, the figure of Javad came staggering out of the mist.

"I shot it!" Javad cried in panic. He was shivering with fear.

"What?" Ahmet Ali seized the Azeri by the shoulder.

"I shot a mountain man! I am cursed!"

Hearing this, the other men became agitated. Some began to curse, while others threw themselves on the ground, prostrating in fearful expectation of the wrath to come.

"Pull yourself together, Javad!" But it was too late. Javad was trembling like a child. Sweat poured down his face.

Before Ahmet Ali could utter another word, another deep rumbling was heard up on the Mountain. The men stood, looking up in fear. The fog hung thick around them. The rumbling grew stronger, and the ground began to shake. Without warning, a huge bolder came hurtling through their midst. Javad's muscles froze. He stood, rooted to the spot. The captain dived to one side just as the immense rock smashed through the remainder of the patrol. Panic broke loose. There were cries and curses as men were crushed beneath its weight. This was followed by a sound like a thousand charging horses as more boulders came crashing down. Then, in the span of mere seconds, it was finished. There was a deathly silence.

Ahmet Ali had escaped the avalanche. But his men had either fled or had the life crushed out of them. Javad's mangled body lay crumbled where he had previously stood. Vugor was nowhere to be seen.

Ahmet Ali was in a daze. He had lost his best scouts, and the remainder of the patrol had dispersed in panic. Alone on the Mountain, he could not go on any further. It was futile. All he could do now was make his way back down the track. It was now nightfall. He had no hope now of finding the plane, and he had no way of explaining to the authorities why he had lost so many men. There had not even been a skirmish. Captain Ahmet Ali had disgraced himself. He could only await the punishment to come. *Was this my kismet after all?* He found some shelter under a lone juniper tree that had managed somehow to find a foothold in the rocky scree. He snuggled against its trunk and wrapped his cloak around his shoulders. He felt for his revolver. It had gone. He must have lost it in the avalanche, although he did not recall dropping it. The loss of his Smith and Wesson was devastating, even more so than losing a horse. It had been his prize possession.

Ahmet Ali tried to sleep. It was bitter cold. He slept longer than he thought he would, despite waking up from time to time, shivering from the bitter air of the Mountain. Frost glistened on the surrounding rocks. The only compensation was that there was no wind. In his physical and mental state, he realized that if he went back to sleep, he might die of exposure. *Better to stay awake.*

He got to his feet and stamped them to drive off the cold. He felt sick in the depth of his stomach. *All is lost. It is finished. There is no point in staying here to die of exposure, but where will I go when I get off the Mountain?* He flung his fur-lined cape around his shoulders and set off down the track. He tried to recall his earlier mood of courage. But the cold hour before daylight was not the time for bravery. It was the hour when men were executed. This was the time when the condemned, having passed beyond all hope, were now resigned to the inevitable.

As he continued the descent, the fog began to lift. He walked slowly down the track, like a man going to the gallows. As he turned a sharp bend in the track, he saw that dawn was breaking over the Mountain. A few yards further down the track, a figure was standing, barring the way. It was an armed Kurd.

Ahmet Ali stopped. The captain's face registered resignation, more than fear; resignation, not because he failed to understand his destiny, but because he did understand. There was a motionless instant in time. In that instant, he relived the Battle of Kars, the smiling face of General Mahmud Mukhtar Pasha as he pinned the medal on his breast. He even relived his childhood. He saw his doting mother and felt the leather belt of a harsh father—not a happy childhood. He remembered with fond thoughts his prize possession—the Smith and Wesson .44 that he had polished with pride. This was his life. And this, he knew, was the end. *This was my kismet*, he thought, as the bullet passed through his skull.

# CHAPTER
# FOURTEEN

O N HEARING THE scream, Nikolai forgot the danger of the heavy mist and ran blindly along the track towards where he thought the sound had come from. He slipped on the wet rocks and fell several times, but he kept running. Then he saw a figure looming out of the fog and blocking the track a few yards ahead. It was coming towards him steadily, on all fours. Nikolai stopped in his tracks. Instead of turning back, he dropped below the track and hid in the rocks. The creature stopped where Nikolai had left the track and hissed quietly.

Nikolai, filled with fear, began to scramble over the rocks. He was bruised and cut by their sharpness, but he continued trying to get as far away as he could from the creature. Whenever he stopped to get his breath, he could hear its cat-like hiss close behind him. However fast he moved, the creature followed, keeping a distance. Whenever Nikolai ascended, the hissing could be heard above where he was climbing. As soon as he descended, the hissing stopped. The creature seemed intent on keeping Nikolai from climbing upwards. At times, it was so close that he could smell its musty odor. Then, all of a sudden, the creature dashed past Nikolai. He could hear its panting as it swiftly climbed a rock just a few feet from his face. Nikolai crouched lower in response, but the creature had gone.

"What on earth?" Nikolai said aloud. Well, whatever the intent of the creature, it was not interested in harming him. All the same, he had the strong impression that it was herding him towards some prescribed destination. Now it had leapt ahead. *Should I follow it?* Reason was telling him to get out of there as quickly as possible. But his instinct was saying to follow it now!

Nikolai walked in what he thought was a straight line, scrambling up and over large boulders until he came to a level goat path. This he followed for some minutes. *Still no sign of the creature. Is it really gone?* All the same, Nikolai headed in the direction that he thought the creature had gone. Against all reason, he knew that he should follow it. The path turned sharply and stopped abruptly at the entrance to a cave. The opening was big enough to admit his SB-6. Curiosity got the better of him. Nikolai went inside and froze. Human bones were scattered on the floor of the cave. Further in, he could see skulls. Were these the victims of ferocious beasts? Or more to the point, were they remnants of meals enjoyed by the creature? Perhaps it was lurking further inside, waiting for Nikolai to go further into its lair. Without considering this any further, he turned and ran out of the cave. He wanted to climb. He had an urge to get up off the goat path. Seeing some rocks that jutted out of the side of the cave entrance, Nikolai scaled the entrance of the cave and found himself above it. And to his relief, he saw another track, much broader, that led in the same direction. However, this time he was above and well clear of the cave.

Nikolai rose to his feet and listened. Climbing back up onto the track, he was startled by a rumbling high up on the Mountain above him. This was followed by a roaring wind, which in the same instant buffeted him with such violence that he was forced to dive back down into the cover of the rocks below the track. He crouched there while the Mountain convulsed around him, its chronic peristalsis shaking and shooting loose rocks in all directions. Then it was over. As swiftly as the Mountain had let loose its ferocity, stillness filled the air.

Nikolai got to his feet. There was no sign of the creature. It had probably taken off at the first murmurs of the avalanche. The fog began to lift, rising and dispersing into small patches that lingered just above the track. Nikolai pressed on. He felt urgency within. *Will I find Natasha?* He hurried once more along the track. His hopes were soon dashed as he saw that a great chunk had been ripped out of the track ahead. There was a gap of ten to twelve feet. *I will have to jump it. There is no way I can climb across. But how to jump it?* He was a strong swimmer but had barely past the physical test at the Air Force Academy. Not like Bagatev, who was an Army long-jump champion. He flew through the air like a bird, landing artistically in the sand of the jumping strip. Nikolai had barely been able to reach the sand. Nikolai knew that he would drop too short and end up smashed on the rocks below. Besides, he could not risk jumping feet forward like Bagatev always did. He needed his hands out front to catch the edge if he fell short of the gap.

He needed a strategy. He blew through his teeth. *If I try to jump forward, I will drop due to gravity,* he thought. *I need to jump high and forward. I need to calculate a parabola.* He wracked his brain, running through figures to determine the speed of the forward run and the speed of the upward thrust needed to clear the gap. He calculated ten feet per second for the run, plus two feet per second for the upward thrust. How he was to measure this was another question. *This is ridiculous. Here I am, faced with having to jump a gap of ten to twelve feet, and I am relying on a mathematical formula to do it. Either I will successfully jump the gap or fall to my death. The question is not mathematical but philosophical.* Nikolai did something he had never done before; he crossed himself. Then he ran at full speed into the jump.

Nikolai landed on the edge of the opposite side and immediately slipped backwards into the gap. He made a desperate effort to clutch at a stunted bush that was growing at the edge. As he seized the bush, it came away in his hand. He frantically grabbed at the bare earth, sinking his fingers into the wet mud of the track. At the same time, he dug his feet into the sides, the toes of his flying boots barely gripping the rough surface. He hung there, poised over the drop, for a second. Then, summoning all his strength, he hauled himself to safety. He had made it. Contrary to the laws of physics, he lay in the wet mud of the track, with the gap safely behind him.

Getting up, he ran with fresh vigor towards where he had heard the woman's scream. He did not have far to go. There, just beside the track, lay the figure of a woman. Nikolai knew that it was Natasha. "Pray, God, that she is not dead!"

As Nikolai reached her, he could see that there was a bloody gash in her throat, but not deep enough to sever the windpipe. The area was soaked in blood. Nikolai hastily tore off his scarf and, bending down, wrapped it around her neck. "My God, am I too late?" The girl did not stir. Her pale face was lifeless.

Sobbing, Nikolai bent down and lifted her up into his arms. He hugged her to his chest in a desperate gesture to pass some of his life into her. He began to pray, "Spasi Bozhe, spasi Bozhe—God save us, God save us!" He repeated this many times, cradling her lifeless body in his arms, like a mother with a dead child. His mind was wracked with despair. One thing was for certain, he was not going to leave her here on the desolate mountain. But he was too wrought to consider how he was going to carry her all the way back to the cabin. To add to his anxiety, he heard the cat-like hiss of the creature. Nikolai huddled with Natasha in his arms, like a cornered prey, and waited. He did not dare to look up. *If I am going to die on the Mountain after all, it will be here, with Natasha in my arms.*

Agonizing seconds passed but nothing happened. Nikolai looked up. The creature had disappeared again. *Is it mocking me? Is it waiting for me to move and then it will spring and deal a fatal blow?* Nikolai waited. An icy wind began to blow down the barren slope. The fog was beginning to lift. He looked around. The creature was nowhere to be seen. But he knew that it could reappear at any moment.

*Got to get Natasha away,* he thought. He laid her gently on the ground once more. He needed to rest his arms. They felt numb. Turning, he checked the surrounding landscape and then bent down again. He pressed his lips against Natasha's and starting breathing into her mouth. "Lord, please let her live!" he sobbed between breaths. There was no response. He quickly removed his sheepskin waistcoat and wrapped it around her. He knew it was a futile gesture, but he did it all the same. The scarf around her neck was thick with congealed blood. But the bleeding had stopped. Summoning all his strength, he hoisted her onto his shoulder and set out back along the track from which he had come. Then he remembered the gap where the track had fallen away. He would have to bypass it. But how? He would have to climb higher, but with the weight of Natasha's body, he was not sure he could do it.

He had only gone a little way back along the track when he saw that there was a ferocious ice storm below, where he had previously climbed. It totally obliterated the track. Volleys of freezing hail pelted the track below, and thunder shook the slope. He would not be able to pass through that storm. What could he do? As he stood there, he realized that the ice storm was rising up to meet them. The air began to tingle with static electricity. There was a humming, crackling, and hissing sound coming from the granite rocks surrounding them. They began to glow with an eerie, bluish-violet light. The ground under his feet began to buzz. *I have to get out of here, fast.* Nikolai knew they were in the middle of a highly dangerous static energy field. It would only be a matter of seconds before the static would discharge itself in the form of high voltage lightning, frying Nikolai and Natasha in an instant. He forced himself to climb higher across the scree of the slope. Just a few yards above, he saw another track, very narrow, probably used by goats. Panting and straining under the weight of Natasha's limp body, he reached the track and rested. He sat with Natasha's body across his knees.

Even though they were above the storm, he felt ice crystals hitting him in the head. It made him wince. The storm seemed to be inside him. He felt its energy surging through his head and chest. Natasha's hair rose from her face in static. He could feel the energy of the storm surging through her body too. He bent his head instinctively to her chest. "Bozhe moi—my God!" he cried out. He had felt a faint heartbeat. Nikolai was beside himself with joy. His first thought was to get Natasha away to safety. *But where?* The storming was forcing them to climb higher up towards the glacier. But he must not give up.

He began to have a severe headache and felt nauseous and weak. He feared he would collapse at any moment. There was no shelter in sight. Not even an overhang of rock under which they could rest. The goat track climbed almost vertically. It ran up between two huge outcrops of black granite. Nikolai had to use his hands to climb. To do this, he had to balance Natasha over one shoulder and then shift her weight to one side, holding her with one hand. With the other hand, he clutched at the rocky surface of the track and literally pulled himself up in fits and starts. He could not go on like this for much longer. His head began to pound. He started to get dizzy, but he knew that he must push himself to go on. *If I give up now, we will be caught in the ice storm that is creeping up from below.* He felt very helpless and alone. *I've had no experience with mountains like this. Even Andriadi would not have known what to do. Why am I thinking like this?*

The track at this altitude was bordered by steep, rocky banks. They were so steep that the stunted juniper and the oak that grew there appeared to be suspended over their heads, ready to come hurtling down at a gust of wind. The slope beside the track was thickly strewn with trees and boulders, which had fallen in a similar manner. Even as they journeyed along the track, a great rock came thundering down only a few yards away. Nikolai had to stop until the dust had cleared. While he waited, he leaned against the surface of a large granite rock that had become wedged between the slope and the track. He tried to breathe deeper. There was not enough air. *Maybe I climbed too high? No, it could not be that. I am still some feet below the frozen lake where I crashed.* Despite the freezing temperature, he had been able to breathe up there.

Nikolai looked out across the terrain below. Like a whirling cauldron of steam, the ice storm spiraled up towards him. He turned away and looked to the east. It was then that he saw a curious sight. A group of men was steadily climbing up an adjacent slope. At first he thought they were Kurds or his friendly Hasasori, but their dress was different. Some wore gray woolen cloaks, while others wore brown cloaks. They carried packs on their backs and leather pouches on their chests. They wore dark red caps. Each climber wore a bushy black beard and long black hair that flowed in ringlets down his back. Although they were approximately a mile away, Nikolai could see them clearly. They were mostly young men—swarthy, with strong, muscular legs showing bare from the knees. They wore soft skin boots that reached to their calves. Nikolai watched them as they climbed steadily up to the glacier. Then a cloud suddenly rolled down from the glacier and covered them. When it had lifted after a few minutes, the men had disappeared. He stared after them for several minutes. He must be hallucinating, for he had a vague memory of seeing them somewhere before. *This is not possible. Not even the Kurds or Azeris dress in such a fashion.* It was then that he began to vomit. He spewed up only liquid. It had been hours since he had eaten anything. He spent several painful minutes retching. After a while, he felt better but still very weak.

Having rested for several minutes, he got a second wind. He lifted Natasha on to his shoulder with great difficulty and started to climb faster. They were now at the snow line. Just above, at a few hundred feet, Nikolai could see the glacier where he had crashed. He did not want to climb up to the glacier, but he had no other choice, for the ice storm was forcing him higher. The track had disappeared. It was covered by a blanket of snow. Choosing what he assumed was the best climb, he made his way with Natasha across the snow. At the pre-flight briefing he had been warned about crossing fresh snow. There was a danger of concealed snow holes and crevasses. The snow could suddenly give way, causing the unsuspecting pilot to drop hundreds of feet to his death. It was best to avoid fresh snow if possible and cross where rocks were exposed. *But what if the hole is next to a rock?* Nikolai did not remember his instructor covering that possibility. Now he had no choice. The storm was spiraling up behind them, and he had to get up onto the glacier, whether he liked it or not. He walked very slowly, testing the ground before him. *Will it give way?* There was nothing else he could do. *Simeon said that St. Nicholas would protect Natasha. Perhaps the saint will protect both of us.*

They crossed the snow without incident, reaching a rocky slope that provided a firmer footing. Just below the glacier, he stopped to rest. The storm below was clearly visible, but curiously, it had stopped, as if waiting for him to continue. *No, that does not make sense. It is my overwrought imagination.* He was exhausted and fearful. As he surveyed the final ascent to the glacier, he saw what he took to be a large, black rock a few feet above them. Its symmetrical shape, however, indicated that it was not the work of nature, but that it had been placed prominently on the slope by some unknown hands.

Nikolai closed his eyes and tried to refocus. Just to the left of the black rock he saw a figure. Nikolai blinked and looked again. The figure was still there. It was that of an old man with a long, white beard and his hair hanging loosely down his back. He wore a shepherd's cloak. *Could it be Simeon? No. That is not possible. What would the old man be doing up here? And yet, he looks like the grandfather.* Admittedly, Nikolai could only see his profile. The old man appeared to be leaning over the rock, busy with some ritual. If Nikolai could reach him, he might be able to help them. Then to Nikolai's disappointment, the old man disappeared. Nikolai took a deep breath. The lack of oxygen was affecting his brain. *First the strange climbers, and now an old man who looked like Simeon.* He pinched his cheek hard. *I must concentrate on climbing.*

Nikolai carried Natasha to the base of the rock and laid her beside it. There was no sign of the old man; not that Nikolai thought there would be. The hallucinations were becoming alarmingly more frequent. The large, black rock, however, was real. Nikolai saw that it was in fact not one large granite rock but a pile of granite slabs that had been carefully and skillfully built up in a one on two pattern. The base of the structure consisted of two large slabs of stone laid side by side. On these, a larger slab had been laid across the two base slabs. This pattern was continued until the structure reached five feet. It had then been topped off with another large slab. Nikolai figured it was about five feet square. The stones used to build this structure had obviously not been chosen at random. They were skillfully dressed, the top stone being rounded at the corners.

Nikolai removed a gauntlet and ran his fingers along the edge of the top slab. There was a series of indents. On closer examination, he saw that they had been deliberately carved into the surface of the rock. The indents made a symmetrical pattern, like some kind of ancient language. They looked familiar, and then Nikolai remembered that he had seen the same pattern or writing engraved on Mehmet's talisman. The top slab was covered with a thin layer of snow. Nikolai used a gauntlet to remove a portion of it. A few inches below the snow, he revealed a blackened surface. Without thinking, he touched the surface with his finger. It felt warm, as if someone had recently lit a fire on the stone. Nikolai began to remove more of the snow. Now he could clearly see that the slab was not level as he had supposed but inclined towards its center like a basin. At the center, there was a hole, which probably had been used for drainage.

Nikolai turned his attention back to Natasha, who sat curled up at the foot of this strange construction. He bent to attend to her. To his surprise, she was fully conscious. Beads of sweat ran down her face. She smiled as he reached to wipe the sweat out of her eyes. Nikolai withdrew his hand in surprise. Natasha's face and body were giving off immense heat. Despite the freezing air, the rocks where Natasha sat were hot too. Nikolai ran his hands down the surface of the rocks. They were not merely warm, but were hot to the touch. They were too high on the Mountain for this to be a hot spring. Technically, it could not be a magma vent. Lava did not seep to the surface without an explosion. Nikolai pulled Natasha to her feet. There was something unnatural about the structure, and he wanted to get far away from it. *No normal person would build such a structure high up on a deserted mountain. And what was it used for? I don't think I want to know,* he thought with a shiver. Natasha looked up at Nikolai. Her face shone with an inner brightness. Her look dispelled his fears in an instant. He smiled and offered her his arm. She stood for a few seconds, and then took Nikolai's arm. They slowly resumed the climb up to the glacier.

*I still don't like it. The heat was real enough, even if the visions were hallucinations. It was no ordinary rock. It had evidently been carved and placed there for a purpose.* Just above the rock, Nikolai saw an assortment of animal footprints in the snow. The footprints were of a great herd of animals, some very large and others tiny and barely visible, that had passed that way down the Mountain. Nikolai took another deep breath. He needed to find shelter. The exertion of the climb and carrying Natasha had used up his resources. He could not get enough oxygen, and he could not stop hallucinating. He pulled Natasha closer to him. He felt weak, and now it was he who needed support. As if reading his thoughts, Natasha offered Nikolai her arm. She had miraculously recovered. He did not know how, and her grip on his arm was firm and strong.

Together, they finally reached the edge of the glacier where he had crashed. After scrambling up the last few yards of the slope, he was forced to rest on a rock that protruded from the glacier. At his feet, the ice was transparent enough for him to make out the debris and rocks that moved with this vast sea of frozen ice and rock. He could hear it creaking beneath his boots. Natasha sat down on his sheepskin and surveyed the scene. Just a few yards away, he saw the remains of his SB-6 at the edge of the frozen lake. Simeon had been right. As the old man had predicted, there was nothing left of the plane, save for a few pieces of the reinforced undercarriage. The nomads had been busy. Nikolai did not want to dwell upon the fate of his beloved SB-6. It belonged to a past that had evaporated like the mists on the Mountain.

Having rested for a few minutes, they continued to pick their way slowly across the glacier towards the ice embankment he had followed the day he crashed. Making their way along the embankment, they came to the gap. There it was. The immense hangar sat protruding from the ice, its entrance gaping wide and mysterious. He glanced at Natasha, who was staring in amazement at the strange entrance before her. "Come on," he gestured, releasing her arm, sliding across the last few feet of ice, and stepping into the great entrance.

Natasha followed. Once inside, they stopped and waited for their eyes to grow accustomed to the darkness. Natasha took Nikolai's arm. "Wwwhat is it?" she asked.

Nikolai spun around. "You spoke!"

"Wwwhat isss it?" repeated Natasha. Her words were slow and drawn out.

"You can speak!" Nikolai seized Natasha in his arms and hugged her close to him. "Is it possible?"

"Wwhat is it?"

"It's a miracle! That's what it is."

Natasha pointed at the enormous doorway.

"I don't know. But it's a miracle! It's a miracle. You can speak!"

Natasha pulled away and glanced into the darkness of the hangar. "It can't be," she said. Her voice was now clear and controlled.

"What can't be?"

"This place." She turned to Nikolai. "It's true after all." She began to cry.

Nikolai put his arm around her shoulder and drew her in close. "Don't worry. We'll rest for a while, and then we can decide what to do."

"But you don't understand." Natasha shook her head.

"What is there to understand?"

"This place is holy. Don't you see? *This* is the miracle."

Nikolai did not see. "The miracle is that you can speak. What other kind of miracle is there?"

Natasha turned and hugged Nikolai. "This is why this is called a holy mountain."

"Now I don't understand." Nikolai's voice was full of frustration. "Do you know where we are?"

"Yes, Kolya. This is the ark."

Now it was Nikolai's turn to pull away. "It can't be. That's a legend. Nobody believes that," Nikolai hissed through his teeth.

"Look for yourself, Kolya," she said, taking his arm and pointing into the interior of the vessel. Her voice was as real as her touch.

He turned, and without another word, walked angrily into the darkness. He expected to find a wide-open space that could accommodate at least one flying machine, if not a complete aircraft, then pieces of one or another kind of evidence to prove his expectation. But as his eyes became accustomed to the dark, he could see that beyond the entrance, where he expected there to be a large hangar was a wide corridor that appeared to run the whole length of the building. He was forced to concede that it was not a hangar after all; of that he was sure, for on each side of the corridor were partitions made of heavy timber and iron. As he walked down the corridor, he found that the strange building contained hundreds of small rooms, and some rooms that were very large, with high ceilings. "Natasha!" Nikolai's voice came from one of the huge, cage-like partitions of the ark. "Come and see this!"

"What is it?" Natasha rushed to see what he had found. On catching up with Nikolai, she stopped and stared in astonishment.

Nikolai pointed to a fence of great timbers that had been erected across the large room in which they were standing. "This looks like an animal cage," he said, glancing over at Natasha. "The timber is at least two feet thick. What kind of animal would have needed such a secure confinement?"

"An elephant?"

Nikolai stared up at the high ceiling. "This is designed to hold beasts ten times the size of elephants." He pointed at the cage-like structure. "And look at how those beams are interlocked—that's amazing engineering." Nikolai stepped out into the corridor and surveyed the scene around him. "I can't believe it. It's fantastic!"

Nikolai continued his search, with Natasha following. As they walked towards the end of the vessel, they saw light coming from a small series of portholes in the walls just below the ceiling. There were smaller rooms here. In some of the rooms there were tiers of cages with iron bars along the front. They reminded Nikolai of a poultry show he had seen in a country town in the Caucasus. These cages were empty now, but he could imagine the assortment of hens, ducks, geese, and guinea fowl. He could still remember the cackling, high pitch shrieks and honking. An unbelievable noise that made him smile when he thought about it. He further noticed that all the walls of the huge vessel were heavily painted with a wax-like paint, resembling shellac. The workmanship of the craft showed all the signs of a high type of civilization. The wood used throughout was familiar, but Nikolai could not recall where he had seen it before.

After inspecting some more rooms, he had had enough exploration. He sank heavily onto the floor, leaning against the highly polished surface of the wall. Exhaustion had finally overcome him. His mind was a blur. Natasha snuggled up close, resting her head on his shoulder. Nikolai reached for her hand and held it tightly. They sat for what seemed hours, resting and trying to make sense of their situation. They were at least alive, despite the ordeals of the day. The cut on Natasha's throat had been superficial. She had bled profusely at first, but now it had congealed, leaving a remarkably small mark on her throat. She had removed Nikolai's scarf earlier when she sat beside the rock altar. She must have left it on the ground. Nikolai had not noticed until now. But then he'd had enough to think about. The earlier events of the day were difficult to put into perspective.

Whatever Nikolai thought this place was, Natasha knew in her heart that this was the ark, and that amazing epiphany was sufficient for her. She was not interested in the details of the great ship. This was a holy place, and that was all that mattered. With these thoughts she fell asleep.

Natasha dreamt that she had been awakened by the sound of footsteps coming down the corridor. She looked up to see an old man with a long, white beard and thick, white hair that hung down his back. He smiled at her and took her hands. She was not afraid, but she could not bring herself to look at him.

He spoke softly. "You want to marry Nikolai. That is good. May God bless you!"

"But what about Grandfather?"

"God will take care of him."

"But I can't leave him." Natasha suddenly woke up. "But I can't leave him," she repeated aloud.

Nikolai had fallen asleep minutes after Natasha. He dreamt that he was standing in the entrance of the great vessel. He was looking into the long corridor. He could hear the cries of birds and the lowing of cattle. Then all of a sudden an old man with a white beard and long hair came out of one of the rooms. He was carrying a large, wooden bucket. At first, Nikolai thought it was Simeon. He called out to him. The old man turned and glanced at Nikolai but said nothing. He then turned and went off down the corridor. Nikolai stood there, staring after him. After a few minutes, an old woman came out of another room with two young men. They were carrying buckets, except for one of the young men, who carried a bundle of hay. They ignored Nikolai and went about their work. The old man appeared again, glanced at Nikolai, and then disappeared into a room.

Nikolai and Natasha had both drifted off into a deep sleep. When they finally awoke, it was pitch black in the corridor. The portholes were still visible, but the light that streamed through them was from a moon that hung gleaming over the glacier.

"I can't believe I slept so well." Nikolai stroked Natasha's hair with his fingers.

"Me neither."

Nikolai looked around him in the darkness. "I can't understand," he said, blowing through his teeth. Natasha took his hand. "Well…" His tone was calmer. "Well, if it is the ark… how has it been preserved for so long?"

"It was preserved in the ice," replied Natasha. "Like cold storage. There is always ice and snow at this altitude. It couldn't rot, I suppose."

"It is scientifically possible, I must admit." Nikolai paused, and then all of a sudden, he began to shake with laughter. His whole body shook.

"I don't find it funny," said Natasha, taking him by the shoulder.

Nikolai gasped for breath. "It's not humor. It's stress. I laughed the first time I made a terrible landing. Andriadi was not amused."

"Andriadi?"

"Yes, my instructor, God rest his soul. I simply could not contain myself. Some people cry under stress; I laugh."

"It sounds to me like hysteria."

"Call it what you like. What do you expect? Especially after all we have been through today."

Natasha drew closer to Nikolai. "I'm sorry, Kolya. You are right. It's that I don't like you laughing in a holy place."

"You are right too, Natasha. It's out of place. I agree." Nikolai pulled Natasha closer to him. "Well, we are going to have to spend more time in this holy place, as you call it. It's now night out there, and we are not going anywhere in a hurry until dawn."

"What a wonderful place to spend the night," replied Natasha.

Nikolai squeezed her hand. *It's like being in the womb,* he thought. *Thousands of years ago, life was preserved here from the great flood. And then a new world was born.* "Yes, it is indeed a wonderful place to spend the night." They slept until dawn.

# CHAPTER FIFTEEN

THE NEXT MORNING they were awakened by the light shining through the portholes overhead.

"Oleander!" Nikolai exclaimed, slapping his thigh.

"Oleander?"

"Yes! Oleander. It doesn't rot! It's the only wood that doesn't." Nikolai was very excited. "That would explain how this could be the ark."

"Could be?'

"Well, is the ark," Nikolai conceded. "Whatever—this is probably one of the greatest discoveries of the twentieth century!" He stood up and stretched. "I need to take samples. This is going to change history."

Natasha was silent.

"Natasha? What's the matter?"

"You are going to take samples?"

"Yes, of course. I can't go back and just tell them I slept in the ark—can I? I need proof. This is an important discovery."

"After all we have been through, you are talking about the miracle of the ark as if it were merely an interesting discovery?"

"Well, of course it is a miracle, but the world needs to know about this amazing scientific preservation."

"Whether the world needs to know or not, that is not the point. Can't you see that we are witnesses of a great miracle?"

Nikolai blew through his teeth. He could not understand Natasha's attitude towards his excitement. He felt the magma of anger and frustration welling up inside, ready to erupt and destroy all that existed between them. The last thing he wanted was to upset Natasha. Of course this discovery was one of the greatest finds in history, especially if this was, after all, the ark of Noah. He decided he must keep his doubts to himself, and so he chose to change the subject. "Yes, of course, it's a miracle," he said, soothingly taking her head gently in his hands. Natasha responded by closing her eyes. "I just got excited, forgive me." He released his hold on her and bent down to examine his knapsack that lay beside him. If he were to take samples, he would need a knife. *Perhaps there is one in the knapsack that Simeon gave me.* He knew that there was not one there, but he looked all the same. Instead, he found the food that Simeon had given him for the climb. "Here, I have some cheese. The bread is probably stale, but it is food."

"It is food," repeated Natasha dreamily.

"I haven't got a knife," he said, breaking off a piece of bread and offering it to Natasha. "You'll have to help yourself to cheese. I don't have a knife to cut a slice."

Natasha opened her eyes and took the bread. She refused the cheese, and so Nikolai took a bite out of the wedge.

"You should eat some, Natasha."

Natasha shook her head.

"I think we should set out soon. It is already dawn, and the weather appears settled." Nikolai paused. "We need to head back while it is clear outside."

Natasha got to her feet, crossed herself, and offered her hand to Nikolai. He quickly swallowed the piece of cheese in his mouth and took her hand. There was strength in her grasp as she literally pulled him to his feet. Her face was radiant, as if some unknown energy flowed through her. Nikolai stared at her in awe. He could not understand how she had recovered so quickly. They made their way to the entrance of the vessel and stepped out onto the glacier. The bright light forced Nikolai to shade his eyes. It was Natasha who led the way, stepping across the ice as though she was simply crossing a meadow. Nikolai could hardly keep up. His pride would not allow him to ask her to slow down. He slipped and slithered as he followed her. Eventually, they came to the spot where they had climbed up onto the glacier. Natasha seemed preoccupied as she scanned the terrain below, and then, as if remembering the way, she began to descend, taking a different direction from the way they had climbed previously.

Nikolai said nothing. He wanted to ask her how she knew which way to go, but he knew that it was pointless. Natasha was following directions. She walked with a determination and an assurance that left him speechless. He meekly followed, an action he had never done in his life before. Natasha strode ahead, walking as if on level ground, while Nikolai slipped and fought to maintain his balance on the rocky track they were following. After a while, they were clear of the snow line, and the track became easier for Nikolai. Natasha, however, did not slacken her pace nor look back to see if Nikolai was following. Normally he would have been annoyed at her ignoring him, but he did not feel slighted or offended; rather, he welcomed the opportunity not to have to make all the decisions. *Perhaps this was Natasha's turn.* He had saved her and now she was repaying him by setting the pace and by leading the descent, helping him to forget the trauma of the recent events. For this he was glad and relieved that he did not have to worry about their safety.

Reaching a large overhang, Natasha stopped and sat on a flat boulder at the side of the track. She smiled as Nikolai caught up. "Do have any of that cheese left?"

"Yes, of course," replied Nikolai, swinging the knapsack from his shoulder and resting it on the boulder next to Natasha. "I could only manage one bite!"

"Yes, Grandfather's cheeses tend to be jaw breakers. They are made from goat's milk and stored for several months. Highly nutritious, but not kindly to your teeth."

Nikolai laughed. He was pleased that Natasha was in good spirits. He also noticed, to his surprise, that the mark on her throat had completely disappeared. "I'll try some more of the jawbreaker," he laughed. He too was feeling in good spirits. Despite the journey, he did not feel tired. He was glad to stop, however, and spend some time with Natasha before she decided to dash off like a mountain goat once more. "Natasha," he said, putting his arm around her.

"Yes, Kolya."

"I know you love the Mountain…"

"Yes?" Natasha turned to him with widened eyes.

"But I will have to return to my squadron."

"What are you trying to say?"

"I have come to love being with you, but I have to go back soon."

"Yes, I do understand, Kolya."

"Well, what I want to say is…" Nikolai's voice was almost at a whisper. "Would you come back with me?"

Natasha touched his lips with her fingertips. "Do you love me, Kolya?"

"Yes, I do."

"I love you too…but…" Natasha turned away and looked off down the track below them. "I cannot leave Grandfather."

It was the answer he expected and dreaded. He had only recently walked into their lives, and now he was planning to change everything. How could she say "yes"? And yet, he could not go back without Natasha. But what could he say? "Let me at least ask your grandfather's blessing."

Natasha did not answer but got up and idly brushed crumbs from her skirt. She made as if to resume the descent. Then, as if suddenly remembering something, she paused and bent over Nikolai. She placed her arms around his neck and kissed him. As she did this, she unexpectedly lost her balance. Nikolai caught her and held her steady, saying nothing, simply holding her. Her heartbeat was steady and strong. His own heartbeat had quickened. Then, releasing her, he picked up his knapsack and prepared to set out once more. Not a single word passed between them as they began the descent once more.

Nikolai noticed that the summit was clear of clouds, although he knew that might not last for long. Natasha was probably thinking the same thing. She began to double her pace, forcing Nikolai to almost trot to keep up with her. They continued their fast pace for almost an hour. Soon they reached the alpine meadow. Nikolai stopped once more to examine the strange salt rocks. They shone, white pillars against the brown and grays of the surrounding terrain. Nikolai saw his chance to bring back some evidence. He bent down and picked up a piece of jagged rock. He chiseled away at the nearest pillar, easily breaking off a fragment. This he slipped into his knapsack. *It will have to do. At least it proves that an ancient sea once covered this area of the Mountain. It definitely will be of some scientific interest,* he thought. *But I need more proof.* Then he had an idea. At the foot of the white pillars there were cushions of pink moss-like plants. He called Natasha's attention to them. "I saw these when I came this way a few days ago," he said, pointing at the curious cushion-shaped clusters of plants.

"Yes, it's called moss campion. It seems to flower all year round, that is, when it is not covered in snow. Grandfather says that it retains the heat of the sunshine in the dead leaves at the center of the cushion."

"It's a born survivor, then," laughed Nikolai.

"It helps us survive." Natasha stooped and pick a petal from the campion. "You can eat it. The raw root skins can be added to soups. It also has healing properties. I collect it for Grandfather regularly. There are numerous herbs we use for food and medicine. The Mountain, in this respect, is our garden. It supplies many of our needs."

Nikolai had to admit that Simeon's meals were some of the most delicious he had ever eaten. He had wondered where the old man had found his herbs and vegetables. *They are here on the Mountain, if you know how to make use of them.* Nikolai picked several of the pink flowers. Moss campion would show at what altitude he had found the basalt rocks. If only he could have brought something from the ark. He had not. These samples would have to suffice.

As they approached the track that led directly down to the cabin, a small owl suddenly flew across the track. Natasha crossed herself.

"I thought owls only flew at night," said Nikolai, looking to see where the bird had gone. Looking back at Natasha, he was surprised to see that she had turned pale. "Is something the matter?" Nikolai asked, taking her arm.

"Oh, no…it's nothing."

"That owl startled you," he said, looking into her eyes. "But it's more than that, isn't it?"

Natasha bit her lip. "It could be an ill omen. The Hasarori say the owl foretells the birth of a child or the death of a man. I know the nomad women well. None of them are about to give birth."

"So you fear someone is about to die?"

"Yes." Natasha diverted her eyes away from Nikolai, looking at the ground. "It's a pagan superstition, but the proximity of the Otherworld is very real here on the Mountain. There are many things we cannot explain."

"I think I am beginning to become aware of that," said Nikolai, smiling bitterly.

Natasha continued. "The nomads believe the owl is a bird set apart from other birds. It stands on the threshold of the Otherworld, reminding us of the ever-present reality of death."

As Nikolai stood there listening, he wracked his brains, trying to remember some of the folk tales of his childhood. He remembered vaguely about how seeing an owl in daylight was a bad omen. He could not remember which tale. Turning to Natasha, he tried to make light of her concern. "For the ancient Greeks, the owl was a symbol of wisdom and prosperity. It's really just a bird, and rather a fine one at that."

"I know, Kolya. May God forgive me, but all the same, I have a bad feeling."

"Well, our feathered friend should have been roosting at this time of day, not gallivanting about in daylight."

"Yes, you're right." Natasha paused. "But I keep thinking of Turnus."

"Who on earth is Turnus?"

"He was a character in Virgil's Aeneid. He saw an owl when he was fighting Aeneas."

"And what happened to Turnus?" Nikolai was confused by this oblique reference to ancient Latin poetry.

"He was slain by Aeneas."

"I did not realize that you had read the Latin classics."

"Not in Latin of course," explained Natasha. "Grandfather has a number of volumes of Greek and Latin classics in Russian."

"Forgive me, Natasha, but you say the strangest of things." Nikolai was thinking that living here alone on the Mountain was not as idyllic as he thought. Natasha's thinking was strange, a mixture of Christian piety and pagan superstition. No worse than most Russians he knew. But he did not like Natasha behaving like this. "You're..." he stammered. The words stuck in his throat. *You're simply amazing,* he thought to himself. Then, as an afterthought, he said, "Well it was an owl, and obviously they live here whether we see them or not. They are simply a part of nature. For me personally, they are rather cute, feathered creatures."

Natasha said nothing.

They continued their journey. They would be at the cabin in less than an hour. As they turned a bend in the track, they saw a Kurd, standing in the middle of the track. He had his rifle aimed at them. Then he lowered it and called out something in Kurmanji. Natasha replied in the nomad's tongue. It was Kelim. The Hasasori stood for a moment in silence and then dashed towards them, waving his rifle in excitement. He hugged Natasha and began to chatter wildly in his native tongue. Then he stopped and took Natasha's hand. His boisterous manner suddenly changed. He lowered his voice and spoke with Natasha in a subdued tone. Natasha listened, her head bent in thought. Then she turned and glanced at Nikolai, her face was pale and full of fear.

*What is Kelim saying to her?* Nikolai did not like being left out of the conversation, but nevertheless, he waited until Natasha was ready to tell him.

When Kelim had stopped speaking, Natasha turned to Nikolai. "I need to go on ahead, Kolya. Forgive me. Kelim has been to visit Grandfather." Natasha could not hold back the tears. "He says that he is dying," she said between sobs. "He has only a little time, it seems. We need to get to the cabin as quickly as possible." She tried to smile, but Nikolai could read the pain in her face. He had no energy to keep up with her pace, and so he was forced to let her go.

"You go. I'll follow as quickly as I can."

"I need to rush ahead. Forgive me," she said, dashing off without looking back. Nikolai watched Natasha, gazelle-like, speeding down the track to the cabin.

On reaching the cabin, Natasha saw a Hasasori sitting on the veranda with his rifle laid across his knees. When he saw Natasha, he rose to his feet and bowed, making a salaam. Natasha greeted him accordingly. The nomad stared at Natasha in surprise. He shook his head in disbelief and muttered something to himself as Natasha passed him and went into the cabin.

It felt warm inside the cabin after the cold air of the Mountain. *Kelim probably lit a fire to keep Grandfather warm,* she thought. It was dark, save for the lights from the small oil lamps that hung before the icons. Her grandfather was lying on a bench beside the wood stove. He raised a hand in greeting as Natasha crossed the room. His breathing was shallow. Natasha sobbed as she took his hand.

"I'm glad Kelim found you. I don't have much time," he said in a weak voice. He turned to look at Natasha. His face was serene, but Natasha could see that his former strength and energy had ebbed away.

*It happened so quickly. Only a few days ago he was out chopping wood and tending to his herb garden.*

"You will soon be free," he said, smiling and squeezing her hand.

"I don't want to be free. I don't want to lose you."

The old man suddenly let out a cry. "You can speak My Child. You can speak!"

"Yes Grandfather." For a moment Natasha saw a young face beneath the aged countenance.

"My prayers have been answered. Glory to God.... Glory to God!"

Simeon raised his head for a brief moment and turned to look at Natasha. His eyes shone with an inner radiance.

"You will be happy with Kolya. I've taught you to believe in Providence. Well, Kolya has come, and now I am going."

"Don't say that Grandfather!"

The old man's voice was beginning to fade. He spoke in a harsh whisper, gasping for breath in between sentences. "You are closer to me...than my own daughter. It's nobody's fault....It is the fault of circumstances over which we have very little control. I was away in the Army...and she...married and went to live in Omsk....God gave me you instead."

"Just rest Grandfather."

"No. There is very little time." Then, regaining his breath, he continued. "Kolya is a good boy, but he has not learned how to marry his mind with his heart. Help him Natasha—do not judge him."

"I'm afraid of the future, Grandfather."

"I'm afraid, too!"

"But how can you be afraid? You have dedicated your life to prayer—and you are afraid?"

"I do not know whether I will get through the spiritual trials that lie ahead. No one can avoid the prince of the air, whatever they may tell you." He turned his eyes towards the icons. "At the departure of the soul, it is tested. I hope I will pass the test."

"Of course you will, Grandfather," replied Natasha, not really knowing what she was saying. Her life with her Grandfather was coming to an end.

"Pray for me, my child, and don't be sad. I must go, Natasha." He turned his head and fell silent. In the same instant, he closed his eyes and was gone. His soul had left his body before Natasha had realized it. She buried her head in her hands and wept. There was a light knock at the door. Natasha looked up as the door opened. Nikolai stood silhouetted in the doorway. Seeing Natasha kneeling beside her grandfather, he came forward and knelt down beside her.

Nikolai stared in wonder at the old man. Simeon's face was as radiant as if it was lit by some inner light. He lay with his arms folded across his breast. Nikolai turned his face away, unable to look at the old man. It was then that he noticed a strong fragrance had filled the room. It smelled of roses. But there were no flowers this time of year, and certainly roses did not grow up here on the Mountain.

Natasha quietly got to her feet and went to the icon corner. There she lit a candle, which she held in her hand while she prayed silently. Nikolai remained where he was, kneeling beside the body of the old man. He felt the calm he had experienced when he first met Simeon. It was like a fragrance that penetrated his whole body. He felt an inner joy. He was now free to marry Natasha. She would need to time to grieve, but eventually she would accept him. *The old man has blessed us,* he thought. *I am sure of it.*

Natasha remained in prayer for a long time. Nikolai's knees, unaccustomed to kneeling, began to ache. He rose from kneeling and quietly backed towards the door. He did not want to disturb Natasha. *Better to wait outside until she needs me.* With this thought, he went outside. The Hasasori that had been guarding the cabin had gone. Perhaps with Nikolai's arrival, his presence was no longer required. Whatever the reason, there was no sign of the nomad.

Nikolai sat and waited. It was getting dark. Nikolai watched the sun set behind the higher slopes. Previously, he had noticed that the wind got up shortly after sunset. This evening, the air was still, as if the Mountain had paused in respect for one of its sons.

The door to the cabin opened slowly. It was Natasha. She beckoned to Nikolai. "I need you to help me," she said quietly.

# CHAPTER SIXTEEN

NIKOLAI WENT BACK into the cabin. Natasha waited at the door to the cave as Nikolai lifted the old man into his arms as gently and reverently as he could. He had expected the old man's body to be very heavy, for Simeon had been sturdy and solid as a tree trunk. And yet, in death his body was as light as a child's. It was as if his soul and his inexhaustible energy had made up the greater weight of his body. They had gone. All that remained was his lifeless frame.

Nikolai was determined to carry the grandfather in as dignified a manner as he could. Due to the weightlessness of the body, he was able to walk slowly and upright until he reached the place of burial. Natasha followed with a lit candle in her hand. She carried a white linen cloth under her arm. She began to chant an ancient hymn. Nikolai did not understand the words, but he recognized the melody. It had been sung at Andriadi's funeral. It's solemnity had moved him to tears.

He had attended his mentor's funeral in Simferopol. There had been a huge turnout. It had been a majestic occasion. The Preobrazhensky Guards had provided the guard of honor. The guards wore white gloves and white slings on their rifles. When they presented arms, their movement was like a sea of white against the dark blue of their tunics. Nikolai had been very impressed by their timing and precision. They moved as one body—not one guardsman out of line. Andriadi's coffin had been draped in the Imperial flag. It lay on a gun-carriage drawn by four black horses. There were civil dignitaries in their gold trimmings and black tunics, and staff officers covered with medals and wearing brightly colored sashes. The clergy wore their ornate vestments and purple hats. A large deacon with an enormous black beard swung a censer as he preceded the burial party. A choir had been sent from St. Petersburg at the request of the Grand Duke.

Nikolai and Natasha processed slowly to the back of the cave. Simeon had requested that he be buried in the traditional style. No coffin. He wanted his body to be wrapped in a shroud and laid in the bare earth.

Natasha put down her candle and unfolded the linen shroud. She spread it out on the ground beside the grave. Nikolai gently lowered Simeon's body onto the shroud. He helped Natasha wrap the body, leaving the face of the old man visible. Natasha knelt beside her grandfather and placed a small, brass icon of the Mother of God on his chest. She then kissed his forehead and covered his face. Nikolai was struck by the beauty of this simple funeral service. Here in a cave on a lonely mountain, was such tenderness and simplicity.

Together, Nikolai and Natasha lifted Simeon's body and lowered it into the grave. Natasha began to sing the Russian Kontakion for the departed. This was one hymn Nikolai recognized. He did not know the words in the old Slavonic, but he had a good ear for melody. He quietly hummed the chant as Natasha sang. Finishing the hymn, Natasha bent down and scooped up some earth. She sprinkled this over the shroud and then stood to one side. Nikolai bent down and did the same. Then, following Natasha's example, he took large handfuls of earth with both hands and poured them over the body. They finally placed rocks on top to form a mound.

Natasha knelt down to pray at the side of the grave. *She will want to be alone with her grandfather,* thought Nikolai. *There is nothing more I can do for the moment.* He left the cave, went back into the cabin, and sat at the table beside the window. *From now on, it is just Natasha and me. Surely she will return with me?* He rested his head in his hands. *So much has happened. I cannot go back without her. I love her.* Within minutes, Nikolai fell asleep.

He was awakened by a gentle hand caressing his head. It was already dawn. The rays of the morning sun were beginning to touch the tiny window of the cabin. Nikolai had spent the night sleeping at the table.

"Nikolai, I need to sort out Grandfather's things."

"I would like to help," he replied, turning to look up at Natasha. "What will you do with his books and icons? You can't carry them across the Mountain."

Natasha seemed not to hear this question. "No. I need to do this alone. It would be better if you could go to the nomad camp. I will join you as soon as I have settled matters here."

"But what will you do? How will you manage?"

"Please don't ask me. Just go and wait for me there."

"I don't want to leave you alone. I don't want to go through all we have been through."

"Trust God. There will be no problems this time."

"How can you know that?" Natasha's look made Nikolai swallow his words. "Forgive me. I have a lot to learn."

"Go now, and I will follow," she said, kissing him gently on the forehead.

Nikolai had to be content with Natasha's decision. Since their time spent in the ark and the repose of her grandfather, Natasha was a new person, or so it seemed to Nikolai. She had an inner wisdom and authority, which he had not noticed before. *Yes, that is it! She is the granddaughter of this remarkable old man. It is as though she inherited the mantle of the Elder, as the nomads called him. Why am I thinking like this?* Nikolai was surprised at his own reasoning. With these thoughts, he set out for the nomad camp.

It was late afternoon when Nikolai spotted the tents. They appeared as tiny black dots against the deep green sward of the yavala. It would take him at least an hour to reach the camp. The amount of hiking he had done on the previous days was now paying off. He walked effortlessly, his muscles toned and responsive to the exercise. He had never felt so fit in all his life. Climbing steadily up to the yavala, he could now clearly see the nomads about their business with their flocks. But before he could reach the camp, he had to descend into a ravine and then climb up and out on to the yavala.

No sooner had he come over the brow of the yavala, where he had sat with Natasha, than he noticed four gray specks speeding towards him. His heart sank. It was the camp dogs. As they raced towards him, he could see their thick, shaggy coats streaming against the wind. Nikolai had forgotten about these nasty brutes. He would be in great danger if he did not take immediate action. It would be better not to run. He must stand and face them. If he turned, they would tear him to pieces. Nikolai's mind raced. He had only a few seconds to assess the situation and act. His life depended on it. He quickly looked for a sizeable rock to arm himself with, but everything was either too large or too small, and the dogs were almost on him. Nikolai decided on a large rock, and holding it aloft, he waited to face the charge. The dogs skidded to a halt on seeing the large rock he was holding. They barked and snarled, but kept a safe distance. *How long will I be able to maintain this defense?* Apart from the dogs, the whole camp seemed preoccupied. There was no sign of humans around to call the dogs off.

Then suddenly, the lead dog—the big, black brute that had been docile as a kitten at Natasha's touch—yelped and turned away. The other dogs followed suit. Nikolai spun around. One of the little boys from the communal tent stood behind him and was skillfully lobbing stones at the dogs. He smiled, his large, almond-shaped eyes full of merriment.

Behind the boy tittered a gaggle of tiny children. If it had not been so serious and life threatening, Nikolai would have laughed, too. But he was shaken by the attack and by the prospect of being torn to shreds. However, he took the young boy's hand in gratitude. In that instant, several of the children seized his other hand, while others tried to climb onto his back or held on to his flying suit, laughing and chattering. Nikolai bent down and scooped up the smallest child, a girl, and placed her on his shoulders. In this manner, he walked into the camp, bedecked with an assortment of struggling limbs and bodies. The dogs by this time lay dozing as if nothing had happened. The lead dog even thumped his huge tail on the ground as the motley procession passed by and reached the communal tent. It was not until then that an adult appeared. It was Mehmet.

Once inside, the children dispersed as quickly as they had appeared to rescue Nikolai. He looked around. There was the same woman making the bread. She was busy again, shaping the flat cakes of dough. Mehmet beckoned Nikolai to the fire, where an old, black tea pot was simmering on the coals. "I don't know why the dogs fear you, Kolya."

"You're joking, Mehmet. They would have made short work of me if it were not for the little boy and his companions."

"They only attack out of fear," mused Mehmet. He really seemed confused by what had happened. "Perhaps you bring something strange to the Mountain. Forgive me, Kolya, but why would they behave like that?" Mehmet had been brought up on the Mountain. He obviously could not understand what the dogs were reacting to. He had a different relationship with nature, if not an intimate one, or so it seemed to Nikolai.

Nikolai smiled. "Well, I survived, thanks to the children." Then, turning to Mehmet, he suddenly had an idea. "Show me your stone again," he said, pointing at the talisman around the nomad's neck. The young Hasasori took off his necklace and placed it in Nikolai's hand. Nikolai fingered its smooth, dark brown surface. It felt warm to the touch. He tried to recall once again where he had seen such a substance before. It was familiar but not in that form. Then all of a sudden he knew. *Of course, that's it! It is bitumen, a pitch used to waterproof boats.* He decided he would give his last ruble to find some for himself. *There must be evidence of it on the ark.* Simeon had told him how Armenian pilgrims used to climb the Mountain to collect pitch from the ark. They believed it had healing properties and could protect the wearer from storms and floods. *I will need to climb up to the glacier once more to collect some. It is well worth the effort. Just think. I will bring back some substantial scientific evidence. Better not to tell Natasha,* he thought. "Mehmet. I would like to go up to the glacier."

"What for, Kolya?"

"To find some of the stone you are wearing."

"I'll go and ask Kelim. He is at the sheep pens at this moment." Then Mehmet added, "He is the guardian of the Mountain." Mehmet got up and went to look for the nomad chief.

Nikolai did not like the idea of seeking permission to climb up to the ark. Kelim might not agree. However, it was not to be a matter of agreement. When Mehmet returned, the answer was not what Nikolai expected.

"Kelim says that it is not the will of Allah."

"Why ever not?" Nikolai feared that might be the answer. But what came as a shock was Mehmet's further explanation.

The young Hasasori continued slowly, as if he was reciting what he had been told to say to Nikolai. There was an embarrassed look on Mehmet's face. "Kelim says that it's no point going up to the glacier. He says you won't find what you are looking for." Mehmet paused and looked sadly at Nikolai. "I'm afraid you won't find it, Kolya." Mehmet gazed up in the direction of the glacier. "Last night the glacier shifted. We heard the splitting of rocks and ice way across the Mountain. It sounded like a hundred cannons."

Nikolai stared back in amazement. It took some time for the young nomad's words to sink in. The ark had gone. It was no use pursuing the matter. This was another thing beyond his control. And for the first time in his life, Nikolai acquiesced. "The will of Allah," he repeated gloomily.

Mehmet reached out and touched Nikolai's shoulder. "Let's drink some tea."

Nikolai sat by the fire in silence while Mehmet made some tea. Together they sipped the hot liquid but said nothing. Eventually, Nikolai could sit there no longer. He had to do something. He got to his feet and made for the entrance of the tent.

"Kolya!" called Mehmet. "It is very important to have what you seek?"

Nikolai spun around on his heels. Mehmet was smiling. "Of course it is. To find such a treasure, such a scientific artifact…" Nikolai's voice trailed off. How could Mehmet know what he was talking about? He did not even know the word for stone in Russian. Yet he was intelligent and engaging. For all his lack of culture and learning, Mehmet could have been a fellow officer under different circumstances. He had a rare quality of honesty and compassion that even Nikolai envied. *Yes, he is guileless, a rare quality indeed.*

"Kolya," Mehmet smiled encouragingly. "Please take this!" He held his talisman in his hand as he offered it to Nikolai.

For a brief second, Nikolai hesitated, and then closing Mehmet's fingers over the stone, he shook his head in refusal. "No, my friend. It's gone. You keep your talisman and pass it on to your sons' sons."

# CHAPTER SEVENTEEN

NATASHA WALKED BACK into the cabin and looked around. Then she collected her grandfather's books into a pile and placed them on the table. She took down the icons and oil lamps and, carrying them, went back into the cave. There she set them on top of her grandfather's grave. Returning to the cabin, she picked up her grandfather's prayer book and slipped it into the pocket of her knapsack. She left the other books on the table. She then took a goat hair bag off the peg beside the stove and packed it with bread and cheese, slinging it over her shoulder together with the knapsack. Natasha took one more glance at the cabin, crossed herself, and went outside, closing the door behind her. *It is finished. A new life is to begin,* she thought as she turned and headed up the Mountain.

It was already dark when Natasha arrived at the Hasasori camp. Nikolai and she made plans to set out at dawn. Nuri and Mehmet would accompany them. Kelim had decided that. It would take them two days to reach the Russian border.

"We will be safe. Kelim will see to that. Nuri tells me that the Turkish patrol that tried to kill me has been routed," Natasha explained to Nikolai as they sat by the fire in the communal tent. "Their leader, a Turkish captain, was executed."

"Executed?"

"Yes. He was found trespassing on the Mountain. It is a Hasasori custom to execute such violators." Natasha paused. "Although, I don't approve of such brutality."

"Well, he deserved what he got."

Natasha looked hard at Nikolai, a thing she had never done before.

"Well, he did order your execution, didn't he?"

"Let's forgive and forget. I don't wish to dwell on it. It's in God's hands. We need to move on, Kolya. We are both out of danger and among trusted friends."

"I am sorry. I am not as used to accepting things as you are."

Natasha touched his cheek. "We both have a lot to learn, and God willing, the years ahead to do this."

"I know we will make it. But it still worries me that a huge Turkish army will be amassed at the border. There could be several divisions. I don't see how we are going to cross without incident."

Natasha said nothing.

At that moment, Nuri entered the tent. He spoke something to Natasha and grinned at Nikolai.

After Nuri had left, Nikolai addressed Natasha quietly. "Are you sure Nuri is trustworthy?"

"He does look like a brigand, I admit. And I suppose he is a brigand. But he is on our side. Remember, I have lived on this Mountain for many years. I know these people. They are my family."

Nikolai would have to be content with Natasha's answer. He did not like the way Nuri looked at them. *Does he have alternative plans?*

At the break of dawn, they set out. Nuri led the way, with Mehmet bringing up the rear. The Hasasori carried knapsacks; old flint-lock rifles; and short, curved scimitars. Nikolai had abandoned his flying overalls for a nomad sheepskin jacket and baggy pantaloons. All that remained of his Imperial Air Force uniform were his flying boots. He and Natasha carried knapsacks, stuffed with as much food as they would need for the two-day journey. They followed an assortment of paths that twisted and turned, but they kept to the side of the Mountain. They could see the great plain below. Above them the twin snow-capped peaks glistened in the bright sunshine. *It's like going on a picnic,* mused Nikolai.

After two hours, they stopped to rest by a mountain stream. As they sat to drink and eat a little of their provisions, which consisted of water, bread, and cheese, Nuri held up his hand.

"What's up?" whispered Nikolai, turning to Natasha.

Natasha put her hand on Nikolai's lips. One minute Mehmet was sitting across from Nikolai, and the next he had disappeared.

"Where did he go?" Nikolai knew he should be silent, but for some reason, his nerves would not let him. Natasha took his hand and squeezed it. *Yes, bite it if you have to, my darling,* he thought. It was too good to be true. They had been walking along the Mountain paths in the bright sunshine with all the trauma of the past days safely behind them, and then suddenly, something had turned up. A something that Nikolai did not want to have to think about. He lowered his head and shut his eyes. The Hasasori were the masters here. He had better be quiet and compliant.

"They've gone," said Mehmet in Russian. He looked at Nikolai and laughed. "The Kurds keep their distance. They won't come near us again."

Nuri, guessing what Mehmet had said in Russian, laughed and indicated that they should move on.

"How many were there?" There was anxiety in Nikolai's voice.

"Not enough to worry about."

"Yes but how many?"

"Mehmet didn't say." Natasha laughed. "Mehmet says they will avoid us in future." Nikolai was not happy with her answer. He could not understand how she could joke when danger lurked on all sides. He met her levity with disapproving frown.

"But what if it had been Turks or their mercenaries?"

"They are ruthless, but not stupid enough to climb up here."

At a sign from Nuri, they set off once more. Nikolai was grateful that the weather seemed to be holding out. Behind them, he could see the mists rising and falling on the slopes where they had had their encounters. Here there was no trace of storm clouds. The ground was dry beneath their feet, and the limestone rocks on either side of the path reflected the heat of the sun. There were no more sightings of Kurds, or even wild animals, for that matter. It seemed they would journey without incident for the rest of the first day.

In the late afternoon, Nuri stopped and held up his hand for silence. *What now?* thought Nikolai. He could see no sign of man or beast. But Nuri had obviously seen something. Mehmet unslung his rifle and cocked the hammer. Nikolai glanced at Natasha. She was too busy staring ahead to notice him. Nikolai waited to see what would happen next. Nuri had drawn his scimitar and was creeping forward, keeping low to the ground. He stopped and waited. Nikolai tried to see what was happening.

Then Mehmet lowered his flint-lock and beckoned to Nikolai. "Look, Kolya, that's a rare sight." He pointed to something just below the path. Nikolai strained his eyes to see. "To the left. It is the same color as the rocks, but you will see it when it moves."

Nikolai looked hard, searching the rocks where Mehmet had pointed. Finally, he saw a movement. Some of the rocks had become liquid and were beginning to ooze down the slope. *What on earth is it?* The rocks appeared to be alive. But they were not rocks—it was the coiling body of a huge serpent. It must have been over forty feet long, with a horned head. It was the same color as the terrain. Any unsuspecting animal or human would not have seen it until it was too late. Nikolai had read about the great serpent of Greek mythology, but had never expected to see one in real life. *Those legends do have an element of truth, after all,* he thought. Looking at the terrain around him, he half expected to see a harpy flying overhead. *But surely, they are just the stuff of legends....I hope.*

That night they camped on a grassy slope, overlooking the great plain below. Mehmet found some dry oak and lit a fire. It was just like the Hasasori camp. Natasha sat and chatted with the nomads in their language while Nikolai was content just to lie down by the warmth of the camp fire and listen. St. Petersburg, flying school, his comrades back in the squadron, his aged mother—they all seemed to belong to a different world. Here on the Mountain was another world. Here on Ararat Nikolai was a different person. *Would he be different when he returned to his regiment?* Of course, he loved and missed his mother. He missed his fellow officers, but for the first time in his life he felt that all this was now behind him. He had not rejected the past, but that he saw it from a new perspective. The ambitious, career-minded young pilot was another Nikolai.

The night was cold, but Nikolai slept soundly, wrapped in a sheep skin that Natasha had thoughtfully packed for the journey. Natasha had been given another long, black shawl. The previous one had been lost when she was captured by the Azeris. She wrapped it around her from head to toe. Only her nose protruded for breathing. In this manner, they slept until the next day.

The sun was already up before they awoke. There was no sign of Nuri. Nikolai climbed quickly to his feet and scanned the surroundings. *Has the brigand gone off to betray us now that we are well out of help from the other Hasasori? Why do I distrust Nuri so much? Is it his ugly smile and close-set eyes? Or is it his general manner? The nomad moves swiftly and silently, like a serpent. He is unpredictable, that's what bothers me.* Yet Nikolai had no real grounds to mistrust the nomad. He had only met him once at his first encounter with the Hasasori. His distrust was purely subconscious. There was no evidence to support his fear. Nikolai turned to Mehmet, who also had just awakened, and asked, "Where's Nuri?"

"Probably gone ahead to check our path. Many things can change in the night." Mehmet stretched and yawned. He did not seem concerned.

*Well, if Mehmet is not bothered, nor should I be,* thought Nikolai. Nevertheless, he waited anxiously for Nuri's return. Finally he asked, "Do we wait for Nuri to come back?"

"No, we can catch up with him. He will have scouted ahead to make sure our route is safe. He will only return if there is a problem." Mehmet reached for his flint-lock. "Better to eat later."

Natasha, who was now fully awake and sorting out her knapsack, took Nikolai's sheepskin, skillfully folded it, and placed it in the knapsack. "Well," she said, readjusting her long shawl, "are we ready?"

"Yes," Mehmet said. "You can lead, Kolya. Just follow the path ahead."

It was hours later when they caught up with Nuri. There were no bandits waiting to capture them or Turkish soldiers hiding in the rocks. Nuri was alone. He smiled as they approached.

"Good. Let's eat." Mehmet threw down his knapsack.

Natasha quickly rummaged through her knapsack, producing some dried goat's meat and a small gourd of yurt. Nikolai delved into his bag for the bread. They breakfasted in silence.

The surprise did not come until late evening. As the sun sank behind the Mountain, Mehmet came rushing back in great excitement. He had gone ahead to scout the path. "You will not believe this!" he said, gasping between breaths. He turned to Nuri and said something rapidly in Kurmanji. The other Hasasori literally jumped into the air and let out an ear-piercing hoot. Nikolai instinctively took Natasha into his embrace. Then the Hasasori began to dance about in a bizarre manner, clapping their hands and striking each other.

Nikolai watched, horrified by the spectacle before him. "Have they gone mad? What are they doing? Tell them to stop, Natasha. They will announce our presence to the whole mountainside!"

Natasha laughed and clapped her hands.

"Have you gone crazy, too?"

Natasha could not answer for laughing.

"Will someone tell me what is going on?" Nikolai hissed angrily through his teeth.

Natasha turned and threw her arms around his neck. "They're leaving. The whole army is retreating."

"What are you talking about?"

"The Pasha's army is heading west. The Russian border will be clear by morning."

"But that's not possible."

"Well, something has happened to change events."

"We were preparing for war. It can't have changed in a matter of days."

"But it has, and we will be able to cross the border in safety."

"But that means my mission, the loss of my SB-6, was for nothing."

"Nothing?"

"Well, not for nothing. But…" Nikolai fell silent. "Oh, I don't know…."

The next morning, Nuri and Mehmet accompanied them to the Aratsky Pass. There was no sign of Turkish troops or of the gendarmerie. The whole area had been abandoned.

As they came in sight of the Russian border, they stopped to bid their farewells to their faithful friends. Nuri embraced Nikolai. Nikolai returned the gesture and then embraced Mehmet. "Be safe, my friend, and thank you for everything."

"May Allah protect you, my brother," replied the young Hasasori.

Both men, in turn, then took Natasha's hand and placed it on their foreheads in respect.

Natasha kissed them gently on the head, like a mother blessing her children.

Mehmet said, "May Allah grant you a safe return!"

Natasha smiled.

"What does he mean a safe return?" Nikolai asked quietly.

Natasha did not answer.

The Russian border was a quarter of a mile from where they stopped to bid their farewells. The Hasasori did not wish to leave the vicinity of the Mountain and so Nikolai and Natasha walked alone towards the Russian border post. There was an eerie silence, broken only by the cry of wheatears. As they passed the Turkish checkpoint they saw that it was indeed completely deserted. A lone sentry box stood empty by the barrier, its star and crescent flag fluttering in the breeze. Nikolai took Natasha's hand as they passed under the barrier and stepped into no-man's land.

The approach to the Russian checkpoint was uphill. As they reached the top Nikolai stopped in amazement and took Natasha's arm. They found themselves looking into the barrels of the latest Putilov 76 mm field guns. They were pointing menacingly at the Turkish side. The gunners were resting by the guns and did not seem to notice the new arrivals standing a few feet away. Then suddenly conscious of their presence, a bombardier looked up and quickly got to his feet. He drew a pistol and challenged them.

"Halt! Show your papers!"

" I don't have papers. I am a lieutenant in the Imperial Air Force."

The bombardier stared at Nikolai in his nomad jacket and pantaloons and repeated his command.

"Heaven's sake man, call the duty officer!"

Nikolai's commanding manner silenced the guard. He turned and called for the duty officer. Within minutes an elderly captain appeared. He took one look at the disheveled pair in front on him and crossed himself. "Bozhe moi! My God – what do we have here?"

"Lieutenant Nikolai Rostovsky and Natalia Simeoneva."

The captain stared at Nikolai's flying boots.

"Are you the missing pilot?" He turned and looked at Natasha. "There was no mention of a young lady. This is very irregular. I think you had better come with me." The duty officer led them into the guardroom where he offered Natasha a chair.

"I'll phone through to your squadron immediately." The captain paused and looked down at Nikolai's boots again. "Is that all that's left of your uniform?" Nikolai smiled at the captain. "That's all that's left of my mission."

The captain shook his head. "I'll arrange transport to the your squadron. But the young lady will have to remain here for the moment. I will need a full report before I can release her.

"Release her?"

Natasha jumped up. "Don't worry the young lady is not under arrest – but she doesn't have any papers." He turned to Natasha. " –it's just a formality. I am sure we will have everything sorted out by the time the lieutenant returns from his squadron."

"It's alright Natasha. You're in safe hands here. I'll be back as soon as I can." The captain nodded to Nikolai. "I'll put her in one of the cells and guard her myself until you return."

"Where on earth have you been?" It was Smirnoff. Nikolai's fellow pilot almost dropped the glass in his hand. "We thought you had been killed on the Mountain, but I see that you are very much alive." Smirnoff's tone was not welcoming. He had always been Nikolai's rival. "You'd better get out of those ridiculous clothes and get rid of that fungus on your face before the Commanding Officer sees you! "

Nikolai shrugged his shoulders. "My fiancée rather likes me with it."

"Your fiancée?" Smirnoff almost fell off his chair. "I thought you had been on a reconnaissance, not on leave. What have you been up to?"

"Well, first of all." Nikolai pulled up a chair, "give me a smoke, Smirnoff, old chap."

Smirnoff offered Nikolai his cigarette case.

"Thanks!" Nikolai lit up a Sobrany. Smirnoff always smoked the most expensive cigarettes. He continued, "As you know I was selected to recce the Mountain, but I ran into a spot of bad luck and managed to crash the SB-6."

"How?"

"I honestly don't know. But there's more, if you're interested." Nikolai laughed at Smirnoff's amazed expression.

"Tell me everything!"

"Well….let me see…I met an ape-like creature, battled with ice storms, spent the night in Noah's ark, and witnessed the retreat of the Turkish army." Nikolai paused. "There a lot more, if you are interested."

Smirnoff shook his head in amazement. "You realize that you could lose your commission for crashing your plane?"

"I'm thinking of resigning my commission anyway. No more flying into the unknown. I'll stick to test flying, maybe. Perhaps Sikorvsky will have me."

Nikolai paused. "But seriously Smirnoff, nothing will ever be the same from now on."

Smirnoff stared at Nikolai in disbelief. "I don't know what you're babbling about Rostovsky. Have you gone crazy?"

"I suppose I have. No one will believe me. How could they?" Nikolai blew a beautifully crafted smoke ring.

"Now I know you're mad!"

Nikolai did not dispute this.

A gentle breeze stirred the vines on the veranda and the scent of basil wafted up from the garden below. Nikolai stepped out on to the balcony and looked at the Mountain. Ararat loomed large and majestic, dominating the landscape with its immense presence. Its snow-capped peaks glistening against a pale azure morning sky.

*Yes we will be back. But not this year.* Nikolai turned and looked at his sleeping wife. "Sleep Natasha. You have another person to consider now."

After resigning his commission, Nikolai moved with Natasha to Yerevan where he took up the position of manager of the new commercial aircraft company. This was a joint Russian Armenian venture that was now providing a service from Simferopol. Next year he would take up the offer of a flying instructor at the Flying Club in Odessa. But his mind at present was on Natasha and their child. *We will return.* Nikolai crept quietly back into the bedroom. He gently arranged the blanket over his sleeping wife.

**PW**

CPSIA information can be obtained at www.ICGtesting.com

232033LV00003B/8/P

9 781414 115153